POOL

new fiction from
Liverpool
John Moores
University

POOL

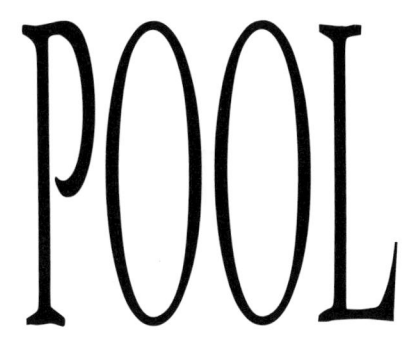

new fiction from
Liverpool
John Moores
University

edited by Maureen Duffy

HEADLAND

First published in 2000
by
HEADLAND PUBLICATIONS
38 York Avenue, West Kirby,
Wirral, Merseyside. CH48 3JF

Copyright © 2000 Individual Authors of stories
Copyright © 2000 Maureen Duffy, Introduction

A full CIP record for this book is available
from the British Library

ISBN 1 902096 75 4

All rights reserved. No part of this publication may be reproduced, stored in a retrieval system, or transmitted in any form, or by any means, electronic, mechanical, photocopying, recording or otherwise, without the prior written permission of the publisher and the authors.

Requests to publish work from this book must be sent to Headland Publications.

HEADLAND acknowledges the financial assistance of North West Arts Board.

Printed in Great Britain by
L. Cocker & Co., Berry Street, Liverpool

Contents

Preface		*vii*
Introduction	**Maureen Duffy**	*ix*
Sight Reading	**Jane McNulty**	*1*
Heart Trouble	**Penny Kiley**	*8*
Nothing Serious	**Owen Liddington**	*13*
The Vanishing Point	**Jenny Newman**	*17*
Chapter of Faults	**Edward Boyne**	*34*
Constant Repetition	**Michael Carson**	*42*
The Character Exam	**James Friel**	*51*
Carcasses	**Robert Graham**	*60*
Parallel Worlds	**Paula Guest**	*67*
Sandpaper	**Jake Webb**	*74*
The Memory of Water	**Helen Newall**	*87*
I am a Bobbie Peru	**Robert Doyle**	*100*
Today We Have Naming of Poems	**Carol Smith**	*108*
Vivien	**Edmund Cusick**	*112*
Saying Hello to the Birds	**Heather Leach**	*129*
An Un-Inhabited Island	**Neil O'Donnell**	*138*
Echo Shoes	**Aileen La Tourette**	*148*
List of Contributors		*160*

PREFACE

POOL is an anthology of short fiction from the Centre for Writing at Liverpool John Moores University. Its contributors are students and staff on our BA, MA, MPhil and PhD programmes. The stories were selected for publication by Maureen Duffy.

Why have we called our anthology POOL? Because the name is a three-way pun on the name of the city, the football pools and the vast pool of talent on which the anthology has drawn. Although only a few of the stories are set in Liverpool, they all share the wit and love of language for which the city is renowned, a city with a famous waterfront and where writing is one of the chief exports.

This is the first volume in a series which will celebrate the short story form as well as the energy and talent of those associated with the Centre for Writing at Liverpool John Moores University.

If you would like more information about our courses, please contact the Course Administrator at the following address:

Liverpool John Moores Centre for Writing
Dean Walters Building, St James Road
Liverpool. L1 7BR

Telephone: 0151 231 5052
Fax: 0151 231 5049
e-mail: j.newman@livjm.ac.uk

Introduction

Maureen Duffy

It's a sad fact of British publishing today that the names which come to mind when you sit down to consider the state of the short story in English are mainly North American, post-colonial or Irish. I put the finger on 'British publishing' deliberately because it's not that there aren't excellent short story writers of UK provenance, or would-be short story writers, simply that, so it's alleged, market forces deny them more than a few outlets, most of them state subsidised in some way. The reaction of mainstream publishers on being presented with a collection of short fictions is likely to be: *Very nice. Now write a novel.* So it's been particularly heartening for me to find the short story alive and well and kicking in Liverpool. As editor of this anthology I've been able to be impartial, insofar as any response to a work of art ever is, because I hardly ever myself write a short story, although my first two serious works of fiction, published in the college magazine, were just that.

If something short comes my way demanding to be put down on paper with pen (as it still does), it will most likely resolve itself into a poem or a one-act play. Of course there's little market for these either. Theatre is about as unkind to the short form as publishing has become but there's still radio and, though much less than there used to be, an occasional single play on television. Poetry has many outlets, including trains and buses, prisons and supermarkets, so it's hard to see why more isn't being done to find a public for short stories. After all, it's a form we have excelled at for at least three hundred years, ever since Aphra Behn published her *novels*, as they were then called, in the days when a novel, as we know it, was a history or a romance.

Before the middle of the twentieth century and the Second World War, it was accepted that professional writers would do their stint of eagerly awaited short story writing for newspapers, magazines or anthologies. Hardy, Conrad, Wells, Bennet, Chesterton: the list seems endless. Indeed it could be argued that for some writers better known as novelists, D.H. Lawrence for example, their best work was done in the short story. Others, like V.S. Pritchett, have written nothing else of great distinction. Would such a writer even get started in today's climate?

Of course there are bolshie writers who persist with the form, often buying the chance of a collection on the back of a novel, and tribute must be paid to the heyday of Virago and its many themed anthologies. But the names that make the literary headlines are mainly those that arrived having been hits at home in Canada or America first: Alice Munro, Grace Paley, John Cheever, Peter Taylor, to pick out a few. A special mention needs to be made of Ireland which has as long a tradition as Britain: Joyce, O'Faolain, Bowen, Lavin, William Trevor, John McGahern and Bernard McLaverty. Again the list of past and present excellence could go on but the truth is that, even including the Irish, the judges of the Macmillan Silver Pen Award for 1997 had only fourteen collections to choose from in what was called a bumper year.

I don't want to depress the skilful and committed contributors to this anthology by over-emphasising the stoniness of the road and the unlikelihood of a crock of gold anywhere along it. We write because we must. My targets are the literary funding bodies and the publishers, but it's also up to us, writers and readers, to see that, what I believe is an important literary form continues to be written and read for its own sake, and every outlet sought for it, including the internet and the multi-media disc. The short story should be admirably adapted to millennial life with its speed, economy and heightened awareness. It should be the form of the future rather than the past and capable of endless mutations, audio, graphic or printed text where not a word is wasted.

The great advantage that we have in writing now is that there's only one rule: does it work? As writers we can, and must, find our own voices, and all styles are there for our proving. The fictions in this collection embody this freedom and eclecticism, from the self-conscious modernism (some would say post-modernism but that's an argument for another day) of James Friel's *The Character Exam*, to the traditional craftmanship of Edmund Cusick's *Vivian*, or from the gritty realism of Robert Graham's *Carcasses*, to Paula Guest's encapsulation of a life and two worlds in fewer than two thousand brilliantly plucked words. Some are all dialogue, others all narrative or interior monologue. Each of those I have chosen has found its own voice.

I don't mean to suggest that other voices, of our predecessors or contemporaries, shouldn't be listened to and studied. The part of writing that is the equivalent of the life class (the recreation of a classic work) or the study of counterpoint is for us the analysis of other texts and how they tick. As a writer you can say goodbye to reading for simple pleasure just as the little mermaid exchanged her tail for walking on knives. Take openings. Openings should grab the reader with the Ancient Mariner's skinny hand and glittering eye. One of the great openers is Katherine Mansfield for the variety and the plunge into medias res of her very first sentences.

Then there are endings. Endings are hell. The fatal temptation is to go on, to add the final paragraph, the telling phrase, the organ music. The classic short story used to have a twist in the tail, an ending that snapped back at itself like knicker elastic. It solved the endings problem but it now seems unacceptably contrived, its very neatness negating what's gone before, like a detective story where the solution is always a let-down. Often all we need is to be brave, cut the last flourish or falling cadence and simply stop. That is Aileen La Tourette's wise choice for the close of her witty and compassionate *Echo Shoes*. And I think it should now be mine.

SIGHT READING

Jane McNulty

As he stood at the gate he realised he'd been rehearsing this for years. Since he'd held Elise, the day she was born, and felt the generations shift, he knew that one day he would stand here. At the gate an overgrown lilac spread its bare bones halfway across the path. Branches, black against the evening sky, dripped rainwater down his collar. He shivered. November, the month of the dead.

In his pocket was a pad of sticky-edged sheets from work. A pen. A key on a ring with a bronze-coloured treble-clef motif. He walked to the front door. Its wood was warped by the damp weather: varnish peeled from its surface like dead skin. He pushed, and the door opened with a shudder.

The place stank of cooker-grease and over-ripe bananas: a whiff of dog came up from the carpet. Smell was the very essence of memory - graffiti for the nose, Braille for the mind. His hand automatically found the hallway light switch. He shielded his eyes. They were sore from a night without sleep, of lying staring into the dark, his nails digging into the palms of his hands. His fingers ached.

He knelt on the fireside rug. Leaning on his knuckles, he could feel the accumulated grit in its pile. There was a box of matches in the grate and he struck one, holding the flame to the element as he turned on the gas. Flames leapt across the grill with a whoosh.

There was a tang of singed dust, as if the fire had not been lit for months. He turned it down until the blue flames popped and guttered.

It had been eighteen months since he set foot in that house, the week following his mother's funeral. It was Easter Monday, sunlight pouring through rain-speckled windows, Mass cards on the window-sill. White rings from glasses left on the table under the window. Freesias dying in a vase of water. He'd gone with Marie to help pack up their mother's clothes for the charity shop.

"It has to be done," she said. "And Daddy won't do it. You know he won't."

He hadn't seen why it had to be done at all. Although Mother wouldn't have needed them anymore, at least the clothes filled the place up a bit: there was something of her left in the house, the smell of her in the wardrobe if you breathed deeply. Molecules of her.

"I've told him we'll do it. Daddy says he's fine with that, as long as he doesn't have to be here himself," said Marie, fidgeting with her buttons.

And now, here he was again. Around the room the boxes were stacked neatly. Marie's doing. She had stuck labels on them, written in her school-teacher's hand, the letters clear and rounded, as if addressing a child. Ornaments, unopened packets of towels and sheets, serviceable pans, the good dinner service from the display cupboard - everything packed carefully. He sat on the fireside armchair and stared at the ghost-white shapes of the cardboard boxes. There was nothing he wanted: he'd told her.

"Put your name on whatever you want," Marie had said to him over the phone the previous evening, "I'll be along after school."

"You can have the lot." He didn't want to talk. There'd been a throbbing pain in his temple and a flashing at the edge of his vision. Migraine - he'd suffered since he was a child and he recognised the signs. Standing in the hallway, the phone heavy in his hand, he could smell the talcum powder his wife was sprinkling on Elise after her bath, and the leaves of the geraniums overwintering on the spare bedroom windowsill.

"We can't put it off any longer, Callum," Marie insisted, "Daddy's paying rent on that house."

"I said I'll come."

"You've not been to see him, though?" There was the hook of a question in her voice, but she knew. She knew very well. "He's been asking after you."

"I've had a lot on."

Marie sighed, softened her voice. "Daddy won't be going back to the house, you do know that?"

Callum leaned his head against the cool of the hall window. "I know. Look, I've got to go and get Elise from her bath. See you tomorrow." He put the phone down. On the glass there was a greasy smudge where his head had rested, with the lines of his skin traced through like a map.

He needed a drink: fumes from the machines at work got into his throat. He went to the kitchenette and pulled down the hatch. Marie had packed most of the pots. All that remained was a liqueur glass, the last of a set with hand-painted flowers. There were dried husks of flies in the bottom. He took it to the tap and rinsed it, letting the water run until it was very cold. When he had finished drinking, he dried the glass on the edge of his overalls and put it into his pocket.

The three-piece suite was going to the Salvation Army, this much they'd discussed. The two chairs were piled upside-down on top of the sofa, their pale hessian undersides baggy as old buttocks. The table in the window had Marie's name on it - the rings would come off with French polishing. She was welcome to it. Everything else could go, she said, unless there was anything Callum wanted for himself. He went out into the hall and up the stairs.

The bedroom doors were all closed against dirt. He pushed open the door to his old room. The bed-frame was upended against the wall, the mattress rolled and tied into a sausage with a length of string which bit into the pink mattress cover. The room had been that way since he left.

What had been Marie's room, at the front of the house, was empty, cleared long since and the furniture taken for her own place. He paused outside the third bedroom, easing the door open. Orange street light suffused the room. He stepped inside, keeping close to the wall, one hand on the door. The double bed was stripped to the mattress, the bedding folded against the bed-foot, the pillows laid length-ways. In the strange light they looked like two bodies lying side by side. He could smell his father's breath, the stink of stale beer and onions. The powdery smell of his mother's skin, warm from sleep. Flannelette sheets. The sourness of sick bodies. The scent of lilies.

"Play a tune for me, son. That Für Elise one I like. You play it so nicely"

"Ah, Mam. It's been years."

She was so wasted there was barely anything of her under the candlewick coverlet.

"Go on. For me."

He'd felt ridiculous, exposed, as if he was wearing a suit too small for him, and the early spring air nipped at his neck and wrists and ankles. His fingers stiff, the notes slightly out of key, he played, while sunlight painted the lilac tree's shadow on the wall above. Once or twice he fumbled, but when he finished there was the sound of thin hands clapping in the room above.

He closed the bedroom door and went down-stairs into the pool of dim light below. He would wait by the fire. To his left, the parlour door stood ajar. A car passed on the road, its headlights sent a rectangle of white light across the room: the lilac tree's silhouette appeared, lengthened then vanished on the opposite wall. There was a sheet draped over the piano, the fragrance of lemon polish in its folds. Callum held it to his face for a moment before folding it and laying it to one side. He lifted the lid. The keys were yellowed, the edges like cracked teeth. He sat down.

It was a hot day. He was eight years old. Out in the street, he could hear the thump of boots against leather, a ball skittering across asphalt. He was practising, training his fingers over scales and arpeggios. His mother stood, a duster in her hand, and her shoulder settled against the door-jamb.

"Now, try your piece," she said.

He took the sheet music from the zip-top bag.

"High wrists." She arched her red hands to demonstrate.

It was the Beethoven. As he played she hummed, nodded time, eyes closed and a smile on her lips. Cantabile. Con Espressione. He had made the music soar and sob and sing. When he had finished, there was a tear on her cheek.

"It cost me my engagement ring, that piano." She wiped her

face with the corner of her apron. "But it was worth it. Just for that."

The notes of the tune trembled in the air. Then with a bang, his father was home. His boots clattered against the kitchen door as he kicked his feet free. He knocked all the air out of the house.

"I might have known you two would be in here." His mouth was smudged with oil and grit from the machine shop.

"He has to practise." She straightened, crushing the duster.

"Why has he? Bloody piano lessons - what use are they?" His father picked up a pile of sheet music and riffled through it. "Here, Golden Boy - let's hear you play this one."

It was in C sharp minor, with sweeping cadences, and peppered with accidentals. His mother edged forward, rubbing his father's black finger marks from the door frame.

"He's not up to that yet. But he's been playing his new piece very nicely."

Callum's eyes swam, the black notes blurred into each other, and his fingers stumbled. He tried to stretch his left hand for the bass chords.

"Jesus! That's an awful racket! I thought they taught them to sight read?"

His mother stepped between the man and the piano. "Leave him, he's only a child."

"What use are lessons if he can't play by sight? Bloody waste of my hard-earned money." His father slammed out of the room.

Ashamed, Callum sat at the piano and cried.

On the box by the piano, Callum's name was written in his mother's shaky hand. He undid the flaps. It was the sheet music. He picked up the top piece and propped it on the rest, positioning his left hand above the first chord. His right hand found the first notes in the treble. As he played the opening bar he knew it: it was the one his father had pushed in front of him that day. In the half light, Callum played the Sonata, the one his mother called Moonlight.

And when he had finished, he closed the lid. Taking a label from his pocket, he wrote his name and claimed the piano.

HEART TROUBLE

Penny Kiley

1972

Mrs K was about to leave her husband when he had his first heart attack. She decided she couldn't leave a sick man and she might as well hang on. He would be leaving her sooner or later.

"Sooner would be better," she thought as she made the bed ready for his return. "Life would be easier without him." And much easier if she wasn't the one to go.

The first time she called the doctor, he said it was probably indigestion. Mrs K wondered if it was her fault. Mr K had complained about the food at dinner time. "Then again," she thought, "he always complains about the food".

The second time she called the doctor, he said it might be indigestion but they'd take Mr K to hospital to make sure. When Mrs K saw him wired to the machines she sensed in one short-lived twinge the glamour of widowhood. It would be more dignified than divorce, and much more convenient. She could stay in the house, for a start.

Her imagination wandered over a house without him in it. She wondered what she would do with the records. They would be the first thing to go. They took up far too much space.

She didn't know why he liked them. She didn't know if he did like them. She just knew he played them far too often. And she often wondered why he had all those Salvation Army ones. "It's not as if he goes to church," she told herself. She went - it got her out of the house - but she could never persuade him to go with her.

The vicar came round sometimes, as they do. Mr K would watch while Mrs K kept the conversation going. For a while, she noticed, he did get better at conversation. Better for him, if not for the listeners. *'My Operation'*, she often thought, "is even more boring than *'What We Did on Our Holidays'*. But at least you don't get the slides."

1973

The year after Mr K's heart attack Mrs K decided to arrange a holiday. She came home with brochures and feigned excitement. "Do what you want," muttered Mr K. She booked a week for two on a Mediterranean cruise. It looked ideal, obviously aimed at the rich and old: people ("like us," she realised) with more money than mobility. She organised passports, travellers cheques and guidebooks. He collected bottles: pills, tablets, medicine.

He stayed on the ship, she went on excursions and reported back. The first time. The second time she didn't report back. The third time she didn't hurry back. All he did was sigh, alarmingly. He said he couldn't walk in the heat: the effort might kill him. She did her best to persuade him.

1974

The doctor had told Mr K to be careful. He could have another heart attack at any time (Mrs K's own heart skipped a beat). No chips, no cigarettes. "You might have to curtail your social life a bit," the doctor smiled. There hadn't been much social life for years.

When Mr K gave up smoking he ate sweets constantly. Otherwise his eating habits stayed the same.

He looked at his plate. "What's this?"

"It's coq au vin, dear."

"You know I don't like my food messed around with." He pushed the plate away.

His face reminded her of their youngest daughter looking at Brussels sprouts, a long time ago. A drop of red spilled on the cloth. It didn't show. The cloth was red too. It was the best one. For visitors.

1975

Mrs K stopped asking people to dinner and invited them for coffee instead. Mr K would sit in his special armchair, at the furthest corner of the room, filling the gaps in the conversation with groans and grimaces.

"And how are you getting on now you're retired?" asked the vicar.

"Tsk," went the armchair.

"Are you enjoying your life of leisure?"

The armchair made a sound like wincing.

"And where are you going on holiday?"

1976

The year Mrs K decided to go on holiday without her husband he threw himself through the French windows.

She booked a cottage for six in Cornwall: herself, her two daughters and her son, her son's girlfriend ("I'll be open-minded," she thought), and a dog. It was perfect. Stone walls, a real thatched roof, an attic room (she gave it to her son and the girlfriend), a five-minute walk to the beach. It was a ten-minute walk to the telephone but she did it every day.

On Tuesday, just before tea-time, Mr K told her he'd had an accident. "I was mowing the lawn and I fell through the glass." He hadn't mown the lawn since he'd been in hospital. They always got someone in to do it.

She packed her bags, gave the key to her eldest daughter and drove through the night. She never went on holiday without him again.

1982

Mrs K had stopped thinking about the future when Mr K had his second heart attack. He was in hospital for weeks.

Miraculously, he survived.

Of course she had to retire. She still kept busy. She got up early, cooked, cleaned, shopped, cooked again and timetabled classes and committees. She got used to the new routine. She had got used to a lot of things over the years. At least, she thought, some of them stopped after he had his heart trouble.

1992

Mrs K was surprised when Mr K died. It was lung cancer, and it was quick. "A few more years and it would have been old age," she thought. She supposed she was relieved.

Before the funeral, she kept busy. She threw out his clothes, his armchair and the bed he died in. She organised paperwork ("I suppose he must have been 72," she told them at the registry office.). She organised relatives.

After the funeral, she felt aimless. She wandered over the house without him in it. She realised she hadn't thrown out his records.

She felt relieved at finding something to do.

She would have to do some dusting. The records hadn't been moved for years. At the back she found something she had forgotten. They weren't all his records. This one was hers. A Salvation Army one he'd bought on their first holiday. It must have been their honeymoon. Written on it was: "To Mrs K (at last!). With all my love from Mr K. March 1952."

He hadn't used the word "love" for thirty years. She hadn't cried for twenty years. She wondered when she would stop.

NOTHING SERIOUS

Owen Liddington

She doesn't love me. It's rollercoaster psychology. I told her. She looked at me like I'm some kind of insect and went back to scratching her arm.

We were happy. Things were fine. Pregnancy was the last thing we expected.

She told me last thing at night. A shitty time to be told something like that. Just as we were getting into bed. She'd been acting oddly all evening - even I'd noticed. She looked like shit, too. I knew something was up.

Alice didn't want the baby. She'd always been against children. Her mother had been pregnant at a young age, her father unknown. I could see her point. It is wrong to bring up a child you don't want. They do know, deep down.

We lay there poached in our own sweat, not speaking. Conspicuously not speaking. Both painfully aware that the other's sleep was a pretence. It seemed disrespectful to fall asleep, as if it would be avoiding responsibility. In that sense, the baby was already there, in the room, demanding attention. We stared at the ceiling together, separately.

Over bleary-eyed breakfast I told her, I just told her, that I wasn't going to let her kill my baby.

She looked at me, shocked. She didn't say anything. She didn't say, I'm shocked. She didn't argue. She looked at me for a minute and then she looked relieved. It was like we'd had a big argument and now it was over. I would have my way. It was all resolved.

So we prepared for parenthood. My Mum and Dad showed us how to work out budgets and act like grown ups. The thing about having a baby is that it takes up all your time and you don't think about anything else. There was a nursery to prepare, clothes to buy, cots and prams to budget for. I didn't realise it at the time, but I was truly happy back then.

Everything was fitting into place. I thought about the time my father had told me that it would. I was seventeen and I'd been dumped for the first time. One minute I'd felt like an adult, the next I was dust. He held my hand and told me things that would seem pathetic if I repeated them now.

Things fall apart. Alice miscarried.

Nothing dramatic. A minor accident. A few hundred pounds worth of damage to the passenger door, a few bruises, not much to see.

I can't describe how I felt. I felt better than Alice. As the shock wore off, I realised what it was I could read in Alice's eyes. I pretended I couldn't see it. She knew I knew. I was too embarrassed to look at her.

She hadn't wanted the baby. Not until.

She hated herself. I was powerless. She blamed everything. I tried to help. She was hysterical. I asked her nicely. She threw an iron at me. I moved out. She wallowed.

I tried to get on with my life. I got out of bed and showered every morning. I kept taking my rubbish out. I worked frantically. What else could I do?

Alice chose the other option. Her days and nights merged. Vodka replaced food. Self-pity replaced sleep. When I went to see her she attacked me. It was pitiful. The way I'd survived proved I didn't care, she said. I must have wanted our baby to die, she said. I was a shit who didn't deserve a child, she said. There was no helping her. She was digging a grave. I decided it wasn't for me.

I worked. I slept. I worked. I found my feet. There is life after miscarriage, I thought. Things had fallen apart around me, but I was still okay. Like a nut with a broken shell.

That's when I got the call. I knew straight away it was bad news. Even as I heard the pulse of the phone, I knew it was bad. I looked at my watch, quarter past four in the morning. Not good.

I drove to the hospital.

Alice had never been very imaginative. I was surprised when they told me she'd used a flare gun. I almost laughed. The flare had set fire to the bed. Nothing, it seems, could get through her thick skull. Our house was just a dusty black shell.

She was shaken. She had a few major burns. Nothing critical, the doctor said. Nothing serious.

She caught me that night. I'd been running away from her for three months. That night, I tripped and fell into the grave she'd been digging. The responsibility I'd run from came down on me like six-feet of earth.

When they let her out of the hospital she refused psychiatric help. She was changed, less hostile.

She came to live with me.

It wasn't what I'd expected. It felt strange. It felt like home. I felt the confused sense of security a homing pigeon must feel when it's put back in its cage.

It's odd. We're together now, but not in a traditional sense. She doesn't love me. She loves self-punishment. Rollercoaster psychology. She tortures herself for the crimes of her parents. I don't think she knows. There's a tragic beauty to it, in a way.

Do I love her? Maybe. I need her. I love her presence in my life. To wake up and feel another breath on my pillow. I couldn't bear to be alone on my own.

THE VANISHING POINT

Jenny Newman

I wish I could fall in love with my colleague, Dr Anthea Mills, who is loyal, motherly, and a leading scholar in her field: the sort of wife most dons dream of.

"The college won't be the same without you," she says, tugging at her cardigan sleeve as she often does when unhappy.

The Master, who disapproves of men who don't marry, omits from his farewell speech any mention my life's work: a three-volume study of the invention of perspective by the artists of the Florentine Renaissance. But the champagne is premier cru, and my colleagues have drunk several magnums to my retirement by the time the scouts start clearing glasses from the quad. On a trestle under the cedar stands my figurine: cast in the quattrocento, it's a generous present even after a lifetime at the richest college in Oxford.

"I'll phone you when I get back," I say to Anthea with whom I've shared many holidays in the past, church-bibbing and gallery-haunting.

"Back? Where from?"

"From Florence," I tell her, as evenly as possible. "My plane leaves at five."

She takes in my linen suit, and my Gladstone bag outside the Lodge with the Panama on top. "Why didn't you tell me?"

"Because I knew you wouldn't like it."

"But I adore Florence - you know I do."

For a moment I suspect that she's twisting my words, but her sheepdog's face is innocent of guile. How typical of Anthea to believe she loves Florence. A city of thrusting towers and rough exteriors, it's always been hostile to women, as she should have deduced from the vain pose of its David, or the snake park of the Uffizi. Even today, with its male bars and spirit of *mammismo*, Florence is a man's city.

"Your taxi's here, Dr Pritchard," says the head porter.

A moustache of sweat forms on Anthea's lip. "You can't go in this heat. It's bad for your health."

Six weeks ago my doctor diagnosed a heart murmur - the result, it seems, of a sedentary life and too much claret. I made the mistake of telling Anthea, who's taken to acting as my nurse.

"Are you staying in the Palazzo Foggini?"

Wishing I'd chosen an hotel unknown to her, I turn away to my bronze figurine, a coquette of a boy with long legs and his skin exposed to the summer air.

"I'll look after it till you get back," says Anthea.

It's a sensible offer, because the statuette's far too valuable to travel uninsured. But a figurine is meant to be lived with and handled every day, not locked away in a desk drawer. And besides, the bearing of this youth is so delicately, pungently sensual that it begs for a return to Florence.

Anthea has already started to swaddle him in tissue paper. Well-used to cutting her losses, she convinced herself long ago that I am shy, an academic bachelor too bookish to propose marriage; so now, when I cover her hand with mine, she goes pink with pleasure. Then her look turns to disappointment as I unclasp her fingers one by one from the figurine's waist, and pop it inside my bag.

The taxi blares its horn. "I'll phone you in a few days," I say, climbing into the back seat. My last glimpse of Anthea is in the wing mirror, not waving but staring at the pale Oxford sun, the tissue paper drooping from her hand.

The terminal is crowded and the champagne has given me a headache. As Alitalia Flight Number AZ237 is lifting off the tarmac, I wish, not for the first time, that I'd lived my life at a Renaissance court instead of an Oxford college. Michelangelo, Leonardo, Raphael. My colleagues revere their genius but censure their love of boys, as though you could have the painting without the passion. As for me, not a genius but a minor art historian, how ever could I tell them about Luca Talentini?

Only when we've crossed the Alps do I allow myself to take his letters from my breast pocket. My students often thought me sarcastic and condescending, but Luca's lack of education tugs at my heart.

"I work too hard to have time for the Uffizi," he wrote to me a few months ago, "earning enough lire to help my family. My sister needs a dowry - and my father as you know is growing old."

It's because of me that he's no longer a rent-boy, so I sent him a money order by return. "Thanks to you, I have moved from my room by the station," he replied a week later, "to be near my new job. The trattoria is very busy."

I wrote back asking for its name and then, when he didn't answer, wrote three or four times at length. His flat does not have a phone, so all I could do next was send another money order, followed by some presents. Still no reply. The forced inaction began to wear at my nerves and spoiled my last weeks in college.

Luca was only sixteen when he first came to Florence as a skinny farm boy. What if he contracted AIDS in those first few desolate weeks - or a terrible drug habit? He might be needing my help.

Which is why, after collecting my figurine from the luggage rack, I'm stepping on to the tarmac in the second hottest month of the year and the height of the tourist season.

Le Cascine. When the sign to Luca's district flashes past the taxi window, I'm tempted to redirect the driver and turn up at the flat unannounced. But what if he's found a new patron - or worse still, a boy of his own age? For a second I see myself from the outside, a foolish old goat in a crumpled suit. It will be safer to check in at my hotel, shower, and go to his flat tomorrow.

At the Palazzo Foggini they have given me my usual room with its faded brocade hangings and little balcony. The only change is a mini-bar, and after dinner I help myself to a whisky. Then, unable to settle, I decide on a stroll. The temperature has reached 93° Fahrenheit, the fountains are spewing litter, and some oaf has painted the David's toenails. I see from an evening paper that a killer disguised as a woman has murdered Gianni Versace, and the sick, sad face of the assassin stares out at me from every placard. Perhaps it's this news of violence and death, combined with my fears for Luca, that draws me almost against my will to the piazza behind the station.

Too timid to approach the boys in their flying jackets and crotch-grabbing jeans, I had wandered here many times before meeting Luca. There was something shy about him, an air of not being quite at home in his body, that emboldened me to stop. He had just arrived from Sardinia, he told me, where his family was living on the breadline. A good Catholic, he knew he was committing a sin - but what else could he do? Leading me by the hand, he took me to a malodorous cubby-hole behind Santa Maria Novella, where I was too nervous to make love but kissed him many times over.

"You have been sent by God to protect me from bad men," he said when my hour was up. "If you will help me get on my feet I need never again work the streets."

Trying to ignore the syringes and used condoms underfoot, I peer at each pouting, upturned face, half-hoping and half-afraid that one of them will be his. Then I drift towards my hotel where the figurine, back in Florence at last, is posing on my dressing-table. On falling asleep I dream of Luca, not in his leathers and number one cut, but floating on a cloud, with the curls of a Signorelli angel.

Knowing his trattoria won't close till late afternoon, I idle away the next day, then take a taxi across the Arno to a modern block on the outskirts of the city. Dear Luca, I think, as I stand on the litter-strewn steps. For him this is luxury.

Talentini. His name is beside the second doorbell.

Pronto, comes his voice over the intercom, high, light and inviting. I push through the scuffed front door and climb the stairs with a pounding heart, then raise my Panama to wipe away the perspiration.

"My God!" Luca is frozen in the doorway of his flat, his green eyes wide. I too am taken aback, because this is not the Luca I remember, but the Luca of my last night's dream, a Signorelli angel with pink cheeks, auburn curls and his tight, ripped T-shirt swapped for a shirt in some silky material.

"*Caro mio!*" I gasp. "How ever did you know?"

I had wanted our lovemaking to be deferred; to spin it out through drinks on the terrace then a long, slow descent into bed, but the shock of pleasure is too great. With one hand clasping his waist, I cradle his buttocks with the other in the way that he loves.

"Stop!" he screams, struggling to disengage himself, "Please, stop." And then, when I grip him harder, he pummels my chest with both hands.

Though wiry, Luca is six inches shorter than me and clearly hampered by his wish not to tear his new shirt. Roused by his feigned reluctance, and my relief at seeing him again, I swing him round and press my lips against his.

"Please!" he shrieks. "You are making a terrible mistake."

His skin smells of fear and cheap perfume, and I see that he's taken to wearing mascara, which to my surprise I find arousing. "Oh Luca," I sigh, tightening my grip.

"Why can't you understand?" he shouts. "This is not Luca. I am Lucia - Luca's twin sister."

Only then do I feel the small breasts squashed against my shirt, and comprehend the reason for the make-up. Stepping back in horror, I stare at the small crucifix round his - her - neck, the neatly-belted waist and patent stilettos. "I'm so - so sorry," I stammer. "Your brother and I - old friends..."

Lucia is panting, and two red spots have appeared on her cheeks. Before I can say any more, she darts into her flat.

"Where is he?" I put my foot over the threshold as she tries to shut the door. "Please tell me, where is your brother?"

"Go away," she says and then, when I fail to move, she lets her hands drop to her sides. "Luca is no longer in Florence," she says, watching my face intently. "And you are - ?"

"Peter Pritchard." I stoop to retrieve my Panama, knocked off during the skirmish. "An English *professore*..." If it wasn't for my need to find Luca, I would bolt down the stairs, never to return.

"Ah yes," says Lucia, looking down at her ripped blouse. "Luca has mentioned you often."

She turns away into her flat, this time leaving the door open. I follow her into a little kitchen where a pan of water is boiling beside a Formica table bearing a television. "Is he sick?" I ask, raising my voice above the noise of a game show.

She only hesitates a second. "It is not Luca who is sick. It is my father. Luca is working the land."

So Luca is back on the farm he hated. "How long will he be away?"

"Until the olive harvest - late Autumn, perhaps."

"Please will you give me his address?"

"You cannot go there." Lucia looks alarmed. "There is no spare bedroom."

"Then I will write a letter."

But Lucia still does not trust me. "I have promised not to give his address. Not to you, not to anyone."

After writing the name of my hotel on my card, I pull out a roll of lire, wondering what, exactly, Luca has said about me to his sister. "Perhaps you will send him this, and ask him to get in touch."

The balcony is festooned with frilly white underwear. Lucia walks to the edge, and gazes down into the traffic. "But you must stay here," she says after a few seconds.

From an unchaperoned Sardinian girl this is an extraordinary act of hospitality, and I stare back in disbelief.

"Please." She lays her hand lightly on my arm. "It is what Luca would wish."

I tell her I couldn't possibly while knowing that I'm going to accept. She is, after all, my only route to Luca, and I sense from her downcast eyes that there's something she hasn't yet told me. Saying

I'll be back within the hour, I take a taxi to the Palazzo Foggini where I settle my bill, and leave my forwarding address.

On my return Lucia beckons me into a room with a snowy counterpane and narrow bed under a Carlo Dolci, never my favourite painter. Turning from his sugary Madonna, I place my figurine on the bedside locker, where its patina gleams in the sun from the little window.

In the kitchen Lucia is pouring two glasses of spumante. Whatever her brother has said about me, it doesn't seem to be troubling her. "To a successful visit!" she cries.

"And to Lucia also," I raise my glass in reply. "Thank you for letting me stay."

After a few sips I begin asking questions, not about her brother, which I sense would raise her guard, but about their childhood.

Relaxing a little, she tells me about their *olivetto*, and the leggy, intractable sheep that roam the mountain-side above it - animals I've heard cursed by the disdainful Luca, but recalled by his twin with love and nostalgia.

"They are so clever, Pietro." Her face lights up. "Each ewe with her own intelligence." Then she makes the money sign. "But Florence is a hateful city. I would not work here if I did not have to."

Her nervousness melted, she starts telling me about the job she's keeping open for Luca, her lecherous boss and the greedy customers - so different, she says, from Sardinians.

"But there's another side to the city," I say and then, afraid she'll misinterpret me, start talking about the Renaissance, the scientists, artists and architects who gave Florence its shape.

"Luca and I are not educated." She points to a pile of gallery guides of the sort sold by street vendors. "They are good, yes? I

24

bought them with my first week's wages."

"Quite good," I say politely, "but it's better to look at the real thing."

"It is hard when you know so little," she says wistfully. "Luca has said you write books about art. Perhaps you will show me some paintings."

Supper is a humble papardelle in olive oil with a few shavings of parmesan which I suspect has been bought in my honour. I retire to bed as soon as I decently can, but am kept awake by the roar of traffic on the dual carriageway. Only as dawn breaks do I fall asleep, to dream that I'm being chased by a giant David with blood red toenails.

The next morning Lucia taps on my door at eight, bearing a cup of espresso on a tin tray. To my surprise she's clad only in her nightgown, a Sardinian heirloom with ruffles round throat and wrist. Beyond her I can see the salotto with a tumble of sheets on the sofa where she spent the night. After more than an hour in the bathroom, she leaves to shop for food on her way to the trattoria. I watch from the balcony till she's round the corner and then, shocked by my own desperation, comb the flat for Luca's address. But all I find is some cuttings from women's magazines, a pair of cowboy boots, some old birthday cards, and, at the back of my bedside locker, a cache of my letters. I scan a few then shove them back in their envelopes, wondering how I ever could have thought he would be interested in my Common Room life.

Late that afternoon I phone my hotel from the corner booth. Yes, I have mail from England, the receptionist tells me in a disapproving voice. Yes, if I wish she will forward it to *Le Cascine*.

For the first time in forty years I have no research on hand, and am beginning to feel bored. "Let me take you to dinner," I say when Lucia comes in from work. "We could start with an aperitif at Gilli's."

"O Pietro," she exclaims, then her face falls. "But I cannot - it is too expensive."

"I shall expect nothing in return," I tell her, adding, when she still looks doubtful, "I promise."

I take her to the places that I longed to take Luca: after aperitifs we go to the Cantinette Antinori, and finally to Badiani's where I watch her devour a *Buontalenti* ice-cream. "Poor Luca, stuck on the farm," she giggles. "How he would have loved this evening."

In her long pink dress she looks more than ever like a Signorelli angel. Not wanting to intrude on her memories, I refrain from saying that the Luca I knew preferred heavy metal bars with video games, and could seldom be persuaded to eat anything better than a hot dog. As we walk home along the Arno, Lucia slips her arm through mine, and at my bedroom door she stands on tiptoe to peck me on the cheek. "Tomorrow I will write to Luca," she whispers, her breath fragrant with Amoretto, "and tell him how kind you are being to me."

"And you must give me his address," I reply as lightly as possible, "so that I too may write to him."

Next morning a fax from Anthea arrives from the hotel. *It's high time I revisited my beloved Florence,* I read in her rounded hand. *And besides, I need to do some research. I have reserved a room at the Palazzo, and look forward to seeing you soon. All my love, Anthea. ps. I will bring your digitalis tablets, which the porter found in your desk drawer. pp.s. I will also bring some mosquito repellent. Do you remember our trip to Venice, and how horribly you were bitten?*

I look round the tiny kitchen where Lucia is making coffee in her night-gown, watched from the top of the television set by the statue of Our Lady of Loreto. How could I explain my presence to the blundering Anthea? She hasn't given me an arrival date, so I excuse myself to Lucia, return to my hotel, tip the concierge 50,000 lire, and tell her on no account to divulge my address to La Signora Mills.

The next day Lucia is off work, and reminds me of my promise to tell her about the great painters. I am too shy ever to have enjoyed teaching, and was glad to leave it behind. But if educating Lucia is the price of gaining her trust, then I'm willing to pay it.

We head first for Santa Maria Novella, on the piazza where I first met Luca, now crowded with tourists instead of rent-boys. I take Lucia round one frescoed chapel after another, finishing with the Trinity by Masaccio, burnt out by his genius at twenty-seven. She's far more receptive to art than her brother, who avoided churches and galleries at all costs, and would pay no heed to my sermons, as he called them. Like most Renaissance artists, I tell her, Masaccio was also a geometer, and one of the first to put his figures in perspective.

She stares up at the fresco. "Please - tell me what is perspective."

"The use of the third dimension." I direct her gaze to God the Father, the most important person in the picture, and therefore at the highest, deepest place. "Perspective was invented here in Florence."

Brighter than most of my former students, she spots straightaway what the tourists usually miss - Massacio's markings still scored on the wall and all rushing to the same spot - the vanishing point or place in the picture to which all lines lead, as though bent on their own extinction.

"I thought great art was about religion," she murmurs, her finger in her guidebook. "But now I see - it all leads to nothingness in the end."

We have lunch in a restaurant off the square, and spend the rest of the day looking at the frescos in San Marco's. That night outside my bedroom door she kisses me more boldly than before, and I sense that if invited she would come in. Though she calls me Pietro, as Luca did, and shares many of his turns of phrase, she's better company than her brother, less moody and more easily pleased. There's a disco that night in the nearby park, and the beat - heavy, insistent, sexual - shakes the thin walls as I lie alone, pondering the freak of fate that drew me to Luca and leaves me unmoved by his far more compatible sister.

The next day I tell her to call in sick, and take her to the Uffizi, where she heads straight for the crowd round the Botticelli Venus. Never having liked the sickly-sweet goddess, I steer Lucia to an adjacent Signorelli. While she stares raptly at the blonde Madonna, I let my gaze stray to the young Baptist in the background with his long, Florentine legs and his buttocks tilted at the viewer. "Just like Luca's, yes?" says Lucia smartly.

Though I draw back startled she gives no sign that she's noticed my embarrassment. "Poor things." She points at the milling tourists. "How exhausted they look!"

The air is stifling, the seats all occupied, and to tell the truth I'm beginning to feel exhausted myself. I coax Lucia out of the gallery with the promise of a shopping trip for clothes, followed by lunch. The strong pound and a lifetime on a good salary have left me with plenty of money. She's reluctant at first, but then agrees to go to Versace in honour of the dead designer.

The windows on the Via de'Tornabuoni are full of tributes, and Versace's is loud with grieving customers. "You have an elegant figure, Signorina," sighs a tear-stained assistant with a glance at

Lucia's long legs. "Just right for the clothes of poor Gianni."

I'm secretly hoping her choice will remind me of Luca - tight trousers, perhaps, or something in leather - but she darts out of the changing room in a flowing creation with frills and flounces.

"O Pietro, I feel so glamorous," she says, running her hands over her hips. "It is the most beautiful dress."

When the assistant smiles at us both I wonder if she's assuming that Lucia is my mistress. The thought is not unpleasant as I sit opposite her that night, watching her dip her biscuits in her Vin Santo. As we walk home along the Arno I become aware of other men's glances: not censorious, as might be expected, given the gap in her and my age, but intrigued and even admiring, as though agreeing I'm a lucky old chap to have such a beautiful girl.

On passing the hotel I wonder if Anthea of the undulating perm and peep-toe shoes has arrived, and what she'd say if she happened to glance out and see me with Lucia, who is clutching her Versace carrier bag and babbling happily in my ear. The moment we reach the flat she dashes into the bathroom to don her new dress. Fatigued by the heat, I go to my bed and lie down. A few minutes later she taps on my door.

"I am growing too plump." She gazes down at her rounded belly. "It is all our good meals."

I force myself to sit up. "You are far from plump," I say politely. "You are a beautiful young girl."

She turns to the figurine on my bedside table. "He is beautiful," she says, stroking the taut buttocks, "more beautiful than me, or anything in the Uffizi."

Despite the ache in my chest, I am beginning to feel aroused. "He was my retirement present from college."

Her eyes stray over the boyish form. "But Pietro, you should keep him at the bank. He must be very valuable."

"Yes - but I like to see him in the city where he was made."

"Do you still love Luca?" She has started fiddling with her watch strap. "Really, really love him?"

I wait till she catches my eye. "Yes," I tell her. "I really do."

"Luca will never come back."

"Never?"

"When will you understand," she cries out, "that he is not able to?"

"But I still don't see - "

"He may be getting married," she is watching me closely now, "to a Sardinian girl."

With its shutters still closed against the heat, the little room has grown stifling, and the pain in my heart is so thick and hot I'm unable to move, or to tell Lucia not to unzip her dress. Clad only in brassiere and knickers, she sits on the bed beside me, the scent from her body musky and cloying. "Why can you not try and love me - for Luca's sake?"

"I wish I could - but it isn't possible."

"I think you would like it," she says, bending to press her lips on the inside of my wrist - a favourite gesture of Luca's that has always made me gasp with pleasure. Then she rests her hands on my shoulders while I try, for the first time in my life, to unfasten a brassiere. She helps me with the hooks and eyes then stares proudly down at her breasts, which are smaller than the Botticelli Venus's.

"O Pietro," she whispers as I ruffle her auburn hair, "this is my very first time. I cannot go too fast."

"I would like to carry on," I murmur, "but I'm too attached to your brother."

"Do you still not recognize him?" she cries, spreading her arms wide, then adds, as I stare in bafflement at her olive-skinned body, "I am your very own Luca."

The special kiss, the knowing ways - how could I have been so blind? I see his urchin's face beneath her smiling one, then stare in horror at the nacreous flesh and the sprouting marshmallow breasts which he's cupping one in each hand.

"Florence is the capital of the sex-change," he tells me. "I have been taking hormones."

"But why, when I loved you as you were? O my Luca - " My voice gives way at the thought of the boy who's been lost.

"I have a woman's soul in a man's body," he announces through painted lips. "And that is why I liked you, Pietro - you were gentle and not too demanding. You would make me a good husband."

I reach for my suitcase with shaking hands. "How can you live such a lie?"

"Because the clinic says so," he wails. "I must live as a woman for two years before the operation."

"You should have told me at once."

"When you appeared I was shocked - because I had stopped asking you for money. Then I thought - why not invite you to stay? I wanted you to realize what I was - but slowly, so you would not be upset. And,' he adds, eyeing me reproachfully, "if you loved me you would help me."

"I can see why you let me dress you," I reply coldly, "but why all the frescos?"

"I am tired of living on a waiter's wages. And besides, they will sack me when they find out what I am. As a *transessuale* I can earn good money as a cocktail hostess for rich Florentines. But only if I am cultured."

My eyes travel down to his penis, lying limp inside his white knickers. Inspired by a surge of pity for its shrunken state, I reach out to give it a timid caress.

"It is a horrible thing," he says, laying hold of my wrist. "Once I tried to chop it right off - but here you can pay them to turn it into a vagina. That is why I want money - the operations are so expensive."

At this my heart begins to pound, and the pain in my chest grows so big that it snaps out of my body and fills the room to its corners, whose contours waver and disappear as I clutch in panic at the snowy counterpane.

Three weeks later Anthea and I are on the plane for London.

"Poor Peter." Anthea looks happier than she's done for years. "What a mess you got yourself into."

I sink back into my seat and shut my eyes. When I open them again a concerned-looking air hostess is offering me an oxygen mask.

Anthea fiddles with the air vent. "It was lucky that I got there in time." It seems that she reached the flat soon after I passed out, and found the front door open. There was no sign of Lucia.

The plane is circling over Florence. Knowing I shall never return, I look down at the roof of Santa Maria Novella.

"A real little opportunist, that Luca," Anthea has got into her stride, "and you too nice-natured to see through him."

Unable to help myself, I glance at the luggage rack.

"There was no sign of it in the apartment," says Anthea. "The police have promised to keep on looking."

"I wonder what the Master will say when he hears it's gone

missing."

"At least you're still alive." Anthea squeezes my hand as the plane banks northwards. "It's good to get these things in perspective."

I can only smile at her dig, to which she has more then earned her right; then I turn, unconsoled, to the night air rushing past the window.

After wasting my life through fear of my own desires, and of what other people might think, I've learnt that perspective is nothing but a sleight of hand, invented by artists for scholars like me, who've deserved to lose my figurine and my Luca.

Now I must travel through the darkness without them to the vanishing point that we all must reach in the end, even those who best knew how to ignore it, and spent their lives in a blaze of ungodly passion for their art and their boys.

CHAPTER OF FAULTS

Edward Boyne

In the sight of God and you, my fellow sisters, I accuse myself. I was careless and thoughtless of the needs of others. I allowed two saucepans in the new kitchen to burn because I was forgetful and too busy with my own concerns.

I prostrate myself in front of you and in front of God. I accuse myself.

I passed on gossip about Sr. Aloysius and her family. I knew it would be hurtful for her and that it was wrong. I accuse myself.

I left the most soiled clothes for sister Bernard to wash. I pretended that the work I did was harder than it was, that I was too old and not able for it. I pretended I was tired. I did this in full knowledge. I accuse myself.

I asked for fifteen pounds from the bursar to buy underclothes and personal things. I went into town but didn't buy anything. I should have given the money back but I forgot and then I became too embarrassed. I pretended I used it for the purpose it was given to me. I accuse myself.

A bold-typed notice was Sellotaped to the scrubbed yellow wall:

AUCTION OF CONTENTS
Friday 4th June at 2pm.

Patrick A. Lynch, M.I.A.V.I.,
Auctioneer and Valuer.

An arrow scratched in blue biro on brown cardboard pointed left at the junction of corridors. Ten paces led to the assembly hall, its doors held ajar by more wedges of cardboard. The early afternoon sunlight streamed into the hall from skylights high in roof. Workmen in overalls were busy moving furniture through another door at the far end. An elderly woman stood by the door sticking number labels on each item as it came in.

In one corner, near a high window with stained glass panels, stood an oak table supporting dozens of crucifixes in various sizes of bronze, silver, gold and brass.

"Looks like the bottom has fallen out of the crucifix market," said Jack Moran, grinning. He exhaled cigarette smoke down through his nose.

Patrick Lynch gave him a look of professional disdain. Moran owned an antique shop on the north quays. He had been taking notes of lot numbers all morning. He wrote down the amount he estimated he could get for an item side by side with the maximum he was prepared to bid for it. Moran had an eye for the margin.

"Convents have a special smell, haven't they? Carbolic soap, wax and stale incense. Are any of the nuns coming to the sale?"

Lynch thought it unlikely. The nuns had moved out months ago. The land and buildings had been sold to a developer for housing.

"Townhouses, you know the sort of thing, "said Lynch. "Fart in the loo and they hear you three doors up."

I sent a letter to an old friend from home without permission. I wanted to comfort myself. I wanted to keep her as a special friend. I did this in full knowledge. I accuse myself.

By one thirty the assembly hall was crowded. A woman tried to open a locked bookcase with a nail file. Another sat in turn on six Victorian hall chairs. She rocked back and forward on each to test the legs. Everywhere was the reddish dark of mahogany, the tattered khaki of cardboard boxes, the dusty smell of dislocation, familiar arrangements broken up and gathered in corners for removal. Near the stage, iron bed frames on castors, empty of their mattresses, were piled on top of each other. On the tables were vases of pewter and terracotta, jugs, bowls, commodes, cups and glasses for holy water, milk, wine, piss.

I gave a back answer to Mother General. I was impertinent and disrespectful. I accuse myself.

Moran had his eyes on two dozen or so religious pictures, some dating from Edwardian times. They had lined the walls of the small chapel and the dark corridor leading to Mother General's office. Cleaned up, he reckoned they could fetch about twelve hundred pounds in all, and should sell here for a lot less.

Moran paused to view a framed photograph of five young nuns in full black regalia.

"Hey look at this one," he said to Joe Delaney who had just come in.

"It must have been taken after they were all ordained or whatever it is nuns do."

"Not worth much," said Delaney. "Pre-Vatican Two, early Nineteen Fifties, sentimental value to someone, nephews and nieces maybe, no more. Nobody wants those stainless steel frames nowadays."

Moran threw the picture back into a cardboard box full of garden tools.

"How is the fireplace business going?" said Moran.

"A bit slow, "said Delaney. "I was hoping to pick up a few old pieces here before they demolish the place."

"Can you imagine living out your life somewhere like this?" said Moran. "All those long cold corridors, everybody praying all the time, up at five in the morning for mass."

Moran sat up on a table with his back to a window.

"It's not as bad as that anymore," said Delaney. "At least, I don't think so. Most nuns these days live in ordinary houses. I have a cousin. She's in her fifties now. She's a kind of social worker. She never wears a habit unless there's a special occasion."

"They give me the willies," said Moran, scratching his knee. "I had them teaching me at school when I was very young. They all had hatchet faces and tongues that could strip paint. We were all terrified."

"That's all in the past," said Delaney who had been half listening. "I'm going upstairs to poke around. I'm looking for a good-sized marble fireplace. I have a customer."

I ate more than my share at breakfast on two mornings this week. I ate bread another sister had left behind. It was more than I needed. I accuse myself.

Moran rubbed the face of a Madonna with his white handkerchief. A black film of grease and dust came away. He rubbed across the bottom of the picture looking for a signature or an identifying mark. Moran had dreams of a Botticelli.

There was the sound of a bell. Lynch liked a theatrical entrance. He mounted a flight of five steps to a small stage. The noise tide ebbed to a murmur. He adjusted his cufflinks at the lectern and said, "Pursuant to instructions received from Sr. Joan Moriarty, Superior of St. Catherine's convent, I hereby declare this auction of furniture and other items open. This sale will be conducted in accordance with our terms and conditions as set out on notices posted near the entrance to this hall. We have a very fine collection of quality items on sale here today. The good nuns have kept everything in tip-top condition so there's value for money to be had. Items bought can be collected at the end of the auction or by twelve noon tomorrow. As always you must satisfy yourself as to the value and condition of your choices as nothing can be returned later."

Lynch started with small items as a warm up. He liked to see his work as a performance, like conducting a symphony, purposefully building to a crescendo. He generally threw in the occasional joke to lighten proceedings but felt wary today.

I went for a walk on Monday evening through Morrow's field. The cattle were in the fields and it was still bright. The sunset was so red and beautiful that I forgot I was saying my office and only started it again on the way home. I became so wrapped up in my own delight that I neglected the consequences and my duty to God. I accuse myself.

Bidding was slow at the start. Some plaster statues and assorted ornaments went for almost nothing. The same fate befell several canteens of stainless steel cutlery. Two lots of iron saucepans failed to attract a bid. Lynch began to wonder if the big crowd had come out of curiosity, wrinkling his experienced nose at the thought.

He moved on to the larger furniture pieces. An Edwardian cabinet which Lynch reckoned was worth £600 fetched only £240. A chest of drawers closed at £60, ridiculously cheap. At this point he tried his favourite joke.

"Items are worth as much as you are prepared to pay for them so it follows that the more you pay for something, the more it's worth".

There was a puzzled silence with just a few grins.

A part of Lynch had always hated the closed faces of furniture dealers.

As a rule Lynch encouraged bids of £10 but quickly dropped to £5 to develop momentum. Bidding was heavy on a set of six mahogany chairs that fetched £405. An antique bureau with a missing drawer handle fetched £700, more than twice the estimate. Two women fought a bidding battle for a solid silver tray. Lynch could feel the sap beginning to rise.

I was angry at God when he took Sister Mary Frances. I thought she was so young and full of life. I didn't pray for two full days. She was very good at the chiropody and she always looked after my feet. I never had to ask her. I was angry at God. I accuse myself.

"And now we have a fine collection, in three lots, of Edwardian and Modern paintings on religious themes. The frames alone are worthy of attention. For the first lot of 8 paintings, do I hear £100?"

I bid £200". It was a woman's voice from somewhere near the back of the room. Lynch squinted in her direction but failed to pick her out. At the front Moran gave his usual sidelong wink.

"I now have £205," said Lynch.

"I bid £300."

It was the same voice. There was a hush and some heads turned back in the direction of the speaker. Moran grimaced. He had hoped for a maximum of £250 but he gave the wink again.

"I have £305," said Lynch.

"I bid £1000."

Lynch could see her now. The crowd around her had parted almost respectfully. He saw an elderly woman in a green cardigan and a white blouse, chalk-faced and frail.

"£1000 going once, going twice-any advance on £1000? Sold."

Moran stubbed out half a cigarette on the floor in disgust.

What's the name?" Lynch asked

"Flynn."

"And now Lot 76, some smaller paintings of..."

"I bid £1000".

The same voice.

Moran fumed.

Lynch hesitated. He tried to think of a way to query whether she had the money to back up her bids. It wasn't some young lad showing off or a drunk with a loose mouth. She sounded very definite and clear. He felt on alien ground, as if there were rules here he didn't know and couldn't understand.

"Any advance on £1000? Going once. Twice. Sold".

The next lot of paintings and prints went the same way. Moran couldn't believe it. He couldn't see her properly from where he stood but some old dear had paid £3000 for a load of musty, fly-blown religious pictures.

I held onto Sister Mary Frances' rosary beads and her missal. I wanted them for myself as keepsakes, to remind me of her goodness and the times we spent together. I told her brother they were mislaid. I told an untruth to him. I accuse myself.

I was angry in myself at Mother General. She told me to kneel on the cold stone floor in the new chapel and pray because she said I was arguing and trying to fight God's will. I was disobedient to her in my heart. I only did what she told me because I wanted to go out to the auction that afternoon. I accuse myself.

CONSTANT REPETITION

Michael Carson

People in the ward keep telling me that I keep saying the same old thing again and again...and I keep telling them that, if I do, it's only because I want them to get it into their heads. You've got to keep telling them. You've got to keep telling them. Constant repetition. It never fails and, if it does, it's not going to be my fault. Not my fault at all. Constant repetition. It's worked for me. I said, it's worked for me.

It's like I keep saying to my son, William.

"William," I say, "get yourself a nice girl who'll take care of you and look after you. A nice girl, William. Your old mum isn't going to last forever, you know. Your old mum's got a shelf-life same as anything else. Mums drop off perches too, you know."

"Mu-u-um," William says, "Don't say that! Please!"

"Have you found one yet?"

"No."

"There you are then," I say.

His chin quivers. "Don't start, lovey," I say. "Tell me about the good old days."

"O.K., Mum. On Friday, January the thirteenth 1989, Daniel Barenboim was sacked as artistic director of the new Opera de la Bastille in Paris," he says.

"Fancy."

I knew I was going to have to gird up my loins. It's my own fault in a way. Ages ago I'd complained about William having no conversation and no idea about history. We can learn lessons from history, I said. World War Two taught your poor dad a lesson he never forgot, I said. And William straight off emptied his money-box, ploughed up our road like a great big ox and bought this huge great big book of dates. And now all he can talk about is dates, dates, dates.

"On Friday the thirteenth of September 1907, The Lusitania arrived in New York after a record-breaking transatlantic voyage of 5 days and 54 minutes," William says, made up with himself.

"What's this bee in your bonnet about Friday the thirteenth?"

"I like to keep topical, Mum...Friday, September the thirteenth 1918, fourteen million Americans registered for conscription."

"Trust them! Those Yanks will be late for their own funerals."

"Friday the thirteenth of November 1981: a bomb exploded at the home of the Attorney-General, Sir Michael Havers, while he was away."

"It was lucky," I say, "that Sir Michael was away. Very lucky for Sir Michael. Nevertheless, not very nice to come home to...very far from nice to come home to."

"Friday..."

"Let's have a little rest, lovey," I say.

"O.K., Mum."

We sit on in one of our two-minute silences for a couple of minutes, and I use the time to think about ways of escape.

I've got my easy chair nicely positioned so's I have a good view of the door to the ward. As they're dead scared we'll wander off they've got this contraption on the door which takes some working out even for the visitors. And that's what I've been studying.

There're these two levers, top and bottom. To open the door you have to pull the top one upwards while you push the bottom one downwards. Then you push the door if you're on the outside; pull if you're on the inside. Anyway I think that's right. Don't quote me, though. I could be wrong.

I.

Could.

Be.

Wrong.

Still, one thing's for sure, once I've mastered it - I said, once I've mastered it - I'll be through that door! Then the whole world will quake at the sight of my fluffy slippers. Bought very reasonably, for a very reasonable and favourable price from T.J. Hughes's's of London Road, Liverpool. An area that is not what it once was. Not what it once was at all. A bit like me.

Like me.

Like.

Once.

"William," I say, at the end of the silence, "William, you ought to find yourself a nice young lady. There're plenty about. I keep seeing them, William."

"Mu-u-um..."

"You're a big boy now, William. You're fifty-four next birthday. Find yourself a nice girl while you're fresh. While your sap is high, William!"

But just then I see Old John heading for the door. Everything else goes flying as the whole ward - those who are half with-it anyway - turn their attention to John in his rude pyjamas with no buttons, making a bolt for freedom. But I know he's doomed. I know they'll drag him back. He can't even crack open a chucky-egg and I reckon if you can't crack open a chucky-egg then you're not going to be able to solve the mystery of the door. And, sure enough, Old John pushes when he should be pulling and pulls when he should be pushing and before long the light and the heavy brigade in the shape of Sister Mary and Nurse Oleander have heard the racket and the shouts of that snitch who gets her hair done every day in return for shopping her kith and kin. We'll get her one day. Trouble is she's well protected; has a private room next to Sister's office. And a natty necklace alarm.

Neck.

Lace.

Alarm.

"Now, John, love," says Sister Mary to Old John, "there's nothing out there for you."

"Where's that jigsaw I gave you to be going on with?" asks Nurse Oleander.

"It's a puzzle," Old John says. Going quietly.

All the drama sends everything flying, of course. William and me have another silence. I offer it up for the boys who died on Flanders Field where the poppies grow row on row. On row. On and on. And I keep wondering if there is a field somewhere, a field. A field anywhere, that has not seen blood. A date in the calendar from the year dot without some wickedness or other. One Pure Date from the very start of things. It doesn't seem like much to ask. That's why I'm here, I suppose. Original sin over and over again, though I know I'm not very original to say so. It's written all over me. Written all over me.

Written.

All over.

Me.

Then Florrie's over. Florrie has adopted me. I know what she's going to say. She'll pinch my cheek and say as how I'm a poppet and a lovely girl and no trouble. No trouble. She's like a stuck record. I keep telling her that she says the same old thing again and again, but it does no good. No good at all. Absolutely no good.

"You're lovely," Florrie says. "A real poppet." She turns to William, who's biting his nails, "She's no trouble. Everyone loves her."

"Sit down, Florrie," I say, but I'm not taking the least notice of her. You see, there's a youngish bloke behind the door with a great big bunch of flowers - a great big huge beautiful bunch of gorgeous big flowers - and he's trying to get in. But he's pushing down when he should be pulling up and pushing the door when he should be pulling. And all the delay alerts Frank who wants to go home to number 17 Talbot Close where, he says, there are two spanking new Sunbeam Rapiers on the drive. He is walking slowly down the corridor, watching the hopeless visitor's battle with the OAP-baffling door. Frank pauses to study a painting of Mrs Horse minding Baby Horse on a windy moor but I know what he's about. He's no culture-vulture. I've seen him snoring through Sister Wendy. And him a Catholic! Suddenly the door yields to the youngish visitor with the flowers. He's through and Frank is striding towards him... up to him...

"Ta, mate," as the youngish visitor holds the door open for him. Not knowing.

We hold our breath...He's gone. We wait on tender-looks for Sister and Nurse. We wait to hear their tights rubbing, their starched skirts crashing creases as they run to get Frank back. Nothing. A puzzle.

"She's a little love," says Florrie.

"Shut up, Florrie," I say. "I can't hear myself hear."

"No trouble! No trouble at all!"

"On Friday, the thirteenth of July 1923, Lady Astor's bill banning the sale of alcohol to persons under eighteen was passed," William says.

Florrie smiles, and William, seeing smiles as a green light, continues.

Now, if Frank had an ounce of common sense - which he hasn't and that's the problem - he'll have gone into the Interdenominational Chapel by the lift, hidden under one of the pews and waited until the heat's off. But I bet you a pound to a pound he'll get distracted by the sweets in the Volunteers' Shop and the good ladies down there will rat on him.

The electric clock - with a chime you know isn't real because it make you think of Dr. Who and that - strikes four. Which means it's quarter past five. Now I thought that was odd from day one. I kept telling the nurses, thinking the daft clock might be a daft test of my sanity, but they looked at me as if I'm daft. I kept at it of course and then I was "Mrs At-The-Third-Stroke", which is not very funny because that's one more than I've had.

"What's that clock ever done to you?" Nurse Oleander asked.

"Don't start me off, Nurse." I said. Cold, cold as community. "Nurse," I said, "Nurse, many of the senior citizens you have here are a touch confused. A clock which strikes the hour at the wrong hour is not going to help matters, now, is it? Is it, now?"

Is.

It.

Now.

I got this blank look back and she took my blood pressure really roughly as if she wanted to wind me up. And I thought, You don't get it, do you? You just don't get it!

Florrie's fallen asleep under the barrage of dates. William is twiddling his thumbs. Well, he needs the exercise.

"Talking of exercise," I say, "go and get your mum a big slab of Dairy Milk from the shop."

He shakes his head. "You've got sugar," he says.

"Isn't it about time you got yourself a bit of sugar?" I ask.

"Mu-u-um!"

"Mu-u-um!" I mimic, just like he hates it. "The main thing is, William, that you're looking after the house. I don't want the place smelling of burnt toast, William. I don't. I didn't buy that smoke-alarm just to remind you that the toast was done, William."

"Mu-u-um," he says, "Mu-u-um, you know I'm not at home. You know they won't let me stay by myself, Mum. I'm in a...another place."

"Well I never! I didn't know that!" I fib. "That's all right then. You're in a home and I'm in a home so we're both in a home and two homes are better than one."

"No, Mum, it's not all right, Mum, it's not all right."

"Hold on! Hold on!" I say so's he won't see me blubber. "They've caught Frank."

They have, too. Of course, I knew they would. An escape takes careful planning. The complicated door's the least of it.

"Don't you worry, William," I say. "Don't you worry. I'll be home and when I'm home I'll bring you home."

"Will you, Mu-u-um?"

"Will I? 'Course I will. Blood is thicker than mortar. Tell me some dates. You don't believe in Friday the thirteenth, do you, William? You don't believe it, do you?"

"Do you?"

"No, I do not, William. I do not. Not while I'm alive and ticking! You won't forget that, will you?"

He nods his head. He shakes his head.

Top lever up. Bottom lever down. Push. Walk...don't run...walk to Interdenominational Chapel, carrying clothes under arm. Lie under pew until the heat's off. Out the door. Number eleven bus.

"Do you want some more conversation?"

"Go on. Go on."

"On Friday the thirteenth of March 1987, Liberal Matthew Taylor won the Truro bi-election."

"Did he?" What the hell am I doing here with him out there without me?

Out.

Without.

Me.

"On Friday the thirteenth of May 1904 the Anglo-Chinese labour convention was signed, permitting the exportation of Chinese to the colonies."

"Tut-tut." Top lever up. Bottom lever down. Push. Constant repetition. Constant repetition. That's the ticket. Just the job.

Sister tells William it's time to go. There's a man waiting.
William tells Sister that on Friday the thirteenth of May 1988, Kim Philby was buried with full military honours. He's got it bad today.

He comes over to kiss me, blubbering.

"Don't worry," I whisper. "Don't worry, I have a plan. I'll be out in a jiff."

William nods, shakes, believing me. At the door he pulls when he should push and a chap outside has to help him. A chap outside has to help him! A chap. Outside.

It should be me. It ought to be me. I'm his mum. I'm his old mum. Push up. Pull down. Push the door. Pull up. Push down. Pull the door. Constant repetition. Constant repetition. That's it. That's the ticket. "Friday, the thirteenth of January two thousand; twenty hundred; oh,oh,oh,; two ow ow ow... Mum comes home to William and everything in the garden's lovely. Everything in the garden's a treat."

Mum comes home!

Mum.

Comes.

Home.

THE CHARACTER EXAM

James Friel

What is your character's name?

It is Paul Sabinowicz.

The 'Paul' is one syllable stretched a yard long in the mouth.

When we were kids and playing at the far end of the street in summer the light would fail and mothers would come to their doors and call us in.

Terr-y-eee!

Jay-mee!

Lee-anne!

Not one of them could reel out a name like Mrs Sabinowicz and wrap it round a child like a lasso and haul him home.

The name Sabinowicz is the legacy of a father who never stayed around or maybe died. All that remains of him is the name mother and son bear like a birthmark or a stain.

How would friends describe your character?

He has no friends.

In this, I can be absolute, having been one long ago. The same age, born two weeks apart, living on the same street and next door but one, I don't think there was a day I didn't spend part of it with him.

I didn't think of him as slow.

I thought of him as lucky.

His mother bought him everything he wanted. He was the first to have a Batman suit, a Spacehopper, Clackers, penny-round collars on his shirts. Mornings he had the choice of seventeen cereals and always a note to excuse him from PE.

When adolescence came, I soared rocket-like away. Eleven years old, I was set One for English, Two for Maths and Paul stayed behind in Mr Ryan's class where all they did all day was colouring-in.

Eighteen years old, I left the place for good except once a year I stay the night and ask my mother how Paul is getting on.

Paul was always anchored, tethered.

In the twenty years since I went away, he has not left the house.

For almost as long he has stayed in his bedroom.

Nowadays he does not even leave his bed.

Like some council house Proust, he lies in a dark room wanking, watching satellite TV and ordering from catalogues high-velocity rifles.

The rifles come in self-assembly packs. There are four of them still wrapped in boxes in the corner.

The instructions fuddle him.

But this year he finally had the nous to put one of them together and it is this, the fifth, that lies greased and triggered beneath his bed.

He's not absolutely sure it works.

How would your neighbours describe your character?

The neighbours haven't seen him for years.

Sometimes my mother asks how he is and Mrs Sabinowicz says, "He's fine, you know, he's fine."

Sometimes she says the opposite, that Paul is, "Poorly. Poorly sick."

This is the phrase I most associate with her and the days when I would call on him and she would say Paul could not come out because he was poorly sick.

My mother says she has made Paul poorly sick to keep him by her and what Mrs Sabinowicz has done is near enough a crime.

And then my mother stops because the next thought is how she has done the opposite - she has a son who never comes home but once a year and not always even then.

So the neighbours, my mother included, if they think of him at all - and they do - think Paul is an idiot, a cretin, and Mrs Sabinowicz is one, too.

Didn't she make the boy soft, marred?

Isn't she paying for it now?

Living in that house with the bedroom curtains always drawn and the smell the milkman says you can whiff just by bending by the letter box.

Mrs Sabinowicz is a fool and so is Paul.

Look deep into that word and there is a line.

A thread.

A lasso.

Throw it far enough and it will haul in *folly, breeze, ghost,* and *love.* Too much love. Too much.

This then is a love story and it ends with a gun.

Who is your character's worst enemy?

I was his best friend and I will never be his enemy. At eighteen years of age I wrote myself out of his narrative and began a story of my own.

I am hundred miles away from him in every sense.

I am beyond his rifle's range.

No, his mother occupies both roles -worst enemy, best friend.

It is her fate to be so targeted.

She is sixty-eight years old and bent into a hoop. She empties his chamber pot, endures his oaths, walks five miles to the chippy on Wogden Way, passing six other chippies because the one on Wogden Way is the only one that does the gravy he really likes.

He insist on this and the long walk is, for her, an exercise of love.

For him, it is an exercise of power.

What is your character's greatest desire?

His greatest desire is to be other than he is but he has not the words.

Eleven years of school and his name's a thing he can hardly spell. The world's a book he cannot read and so he closed it and turned away.

For me, my greatest desire is to be other than I am. For me, the world is text or, when it's not, I turn it into one.

Here is Paul, presented here, made of words by me.

He has other desires, I know. The fondness for mail order is proof of this.

His mother fills in the coupons.

Last year he ordered Gameboys, computer games he could not play to any clever level. The year before, bizarrely, camping equipment.

The goods lie about the house, unwrapped, unused.

His mother fills in the coupons for him and there is a massive bill that monthly she is paying off.

How can she deny him?

He is forty years old and winces at just so much as a glimpse of sunlight.

He is all she has, ruined goods she can't return.

They are in love.

There is gun beneath the bed.

What does your character do in his spare time?

All his time is spare. He has grown fat on it. As a boy he was thin as six o'clock. Twenty years have turned him to a blob.

He lies in his bed, under blanket on blanket, fingering himself and the remote control: images of blood, sex, perfect bodies, battles, bombs and game-shows flit across the TV screen and the larger one in his head where they grow in size, take on dimension. The mail order magazine, *Soldier of Fortune*, advertises mercenary posts in Uganda, Ecuador, Sierra Leone. Muscular men in khaki part jungles, raze the green with machine gun fire and sometimes, increasingly, he is with them, leading the way.

It is eighteen years since Paul Sabinowicz has seen the bottom of the stairs.

There's a gun under the bed.

He thinks it done.

Two screws sit on a full ashtray.

He knows they go in somewhere but the gun looks complete without it.

Perhaps they're spare.

His mother comes in the front door and the smell of chips and gravy reaches the door before she does.

What does your character do for a living?

He fires the gun.

No, the gun goes off in his hands and, so powerful is the reflex, it lifts him from the bed and throws him against the wall.

The bullet powers through the half-open door, winging the latch and shattering the mirror on the landing.

It misses his mother's waist by an inch, a fraction, and seems to create a draught in its wake that propels her down the stairs, tumbling her down the first ten steps.

She crawls like a dog the rest of the way and out on to the street.

It is my mother who hears the shot and sees Muriel Sabinowicz on the far side of the pavement, clutching the lamppost, keening Paul's name, howling at the house.

At the upstairs window the curtains momentarily part and Paul shows his face to daylight for the first time since no one can remember when.

It is my mother who calls the police.

What is your character's greatest fear?

It is this: that he is too small even for the tiny space the world allows him.

In minutes that world comes crowding in and wants him out.

Police block either end of Ridyard Street.

Residents are rushed from surrounding houses guarded by men in flak-jackets who then dodge their way back to 127 and take aim at the upstairs window.

Two helicopters circle in the sky. Their noise adds to the drama.

The glamour.

The comedy.

It looks as if some one has traced a page from the *Soldier of*

Fortune catalogue and held it over the Kenyon Estate.

How will your character develop?

As a boy he was well-fed, glossy, groomed. Then, in a summer, he became a rake, taller than me by a foot. His mother would never let him out looking less than his best. He'd stand in the doorway when I called, shuffling his feet, kicking out at his mother who knelt before us spitting and polishing his shoes, tying up his laces.

Now his mother wails his name through a megaphone but it takes five hours for the police to coax him from his room.

When he finally emerges, TV cameras are there.

His hair reaches in rats tails to his waists.

His fingernails are so long they curl round his fingertips.

He is twenty stone in weight and is carried out by six policemen, handcuffed to a pole.

He wears a string vest and underpants yellow at the crotch.

His eyes are closed and he pretends to be what he has been most of his life but today it's the one thing he is not - that is to say, invisible, a ghost.

He is led into a van and taken away.

For questioning.

What is your character's ultimate destination.

An asylum.

His name features in a series of reports.

No charges are made.

Three days later he is back with his mother at 127 Ridyard Street.

There is a petition at his return.

My mother is the only one who does not sign it.

Over the phone she tells me, "At least he's with someone who loves him. At least he's home. Don't you think? Don't you?"

There is a silence even a Paul Sabinowicz could read.

She wants me to agree with her.

And I do.

I do.

But I don't say this.

I say nothing.

This is one question I will not answer.

This is part of the exam in which I fail to score.

What purpose does your character serve in the overall narrative?

I am drawn to the one detail I have made up, the one thing I know not to be true.

I know there was only one bullet fired and that it burst the door lock.

I have made up the mirror on the landing.

I wanted a mirror in this piece.

I wanted a mirror that was shattered.

I have this theory and it haunts me, that there are lives we do not live, that there are people we almost are and never quite become.

There are choices we make and choices made for us that determine whether we do this or that or this.

It's the things we do not do, the people we somehow never get to be or escape from being who haunt us.

They never vanish. They are never quite invisible.

No. They haunt us. They prosper deep within us until we become a host of shadows.

We feel inside these unlived ghosts, their soft unfurlings.

The heart is such a delicate organ.

If I question myself, it is Paul Sabinowicz who rises to the surface like a face meeting its reflection in a dusty mirror.

I am here because I passed an exam and then another and another. I wrote down all the right answers and my reward is to go on writing and every word is an attempt to silence whatever siren call Paul Sabinowicz heard that made him turn from this world, close it like a book.

This is a love story and it ends with a gun.

Paul Sabinowicz took aim at his mother and missed.

Here is Paul in my sights.

Has my aim been true?

Have I missed?

Have I?

CARCASSES

Robert Graham

Veins turn my stomach. They don't have to be varicose - just visible. Somewhere along the way, I became hardened to decaying flesh. Cellulite holds no further horrors for me. Dimpled, slack, stretched, drooping flesh has been part of life for such a long time. But I can't be doing with veins at all. And the swimming pool is full of them. Tuesdays and Thursdays, week in, week out, I swim. It's free for pensioners then. Nobody looking at us in our clothes could suspect the ugliness hidden beneath. And under the skin - well, who could tell what's there by looking at our undressed carcasses?

Here we are.
There must be fifteen of us on a good day and I know all of them at least by name. Most of us went to the Elementary School together. The streets outside, where we've lived our lives, are dank, Edwardian red-bricks, and it's odd to me that our lifetimes have been passed out there and now we're reaching the end here in the bright, glinting pool, built only five years ago - the day before yesterday, really.
Picture us, crossing and re-crossing the pool - most of us swim widths, not lengths - like sluggardly dredgers passing across a bay.
I'm early today, but I might just as well be late. I don't have any

regard for time - I gave it up. There's a clock on the front-room mantelpiece, but that's all. I don't wear a watch.

The blackboard beneath the pool clock says 83°F in shaky chalk, but it never is. They always say it's that and it's always colder than they say, because 83°F would be warm, wouldn't it?

I'm at the yellow steps, which take you very gradually up to your waist in chilly, sharp blue, but I stop there and look around.

There's Mr. & Mrs. Johnny Weismuller, as I call them - the diving stars. Neither one of them is any younger than me, but they practise and analyse diving like they were in training for an event.

When she completes a dive, never well, he's waiting for her at the side and she'll give him all her attention as he bends from the waist, brings his arms together above his head and gives it some post-match analysis.

They're like a pair of teenagers who've just started going with each other. I don't know how she's put up with a lifetime of that. Johnny nods at me, very formal. Of course, I stretch a big smile back at him.

Nan Morris is in, wading around the shallow end. Her costume's only wet to the waist and there's an empty hollow in it up above, where her right breast should be. I thought they gave you pads to stick in there. I mean, the rest of us have feelings, don't we? Anyway, I don't think Nan's really all there.

I swim a width and turn onto my back to wet my hair. I used to wear a white rubber cap, but I stopped. You wouldn't believe how often I've had people asking about it. Wasn't I wearing a cap anymore? Wasn't I bothered about getting my hair wet? Wouldn't my head be cold without it?

"Look around," I'd tell them. "Are any of this lot dying of

pneumonia?"

Worst of them all was Esta McKeever. She went on and on and I held my tongue as long as I could, seeing as her husband had died not long since. She'd had a bad twelve months, really: they'd amputated his right leg at the knee - cancer - in March and by August he was dead anyway.

I turn and begin a length, which brings me along by Gordon, the attendant. He sits in his high chair, staring without focus and looking like a tennis umpire waiting for a match that's never going to happen. I worry for him. He never acknowledges your presence. In fact, we didn't even know his name until Esta McKeever became a Born Again and found it out.

She'd never spoken to him before. None of us had. Gordon's very interested in the young girls, especially when they're walking about or waist-high in the water, but not interested in anything else. Today, as he very often is, Gordon is wearing a Coq Sportif T-shirt. Very fitting.

Jean Mahoney is sat at the other end, so I make a swift turnaround.

"Iya," is all I say to Jean. She can mither on for as long as anyone will let her, given an inch, moaning away about whatever debris floats across her mind: her husband, vandals, semi-skimmed milk, her new diet or the Germans. I can't listen to it anymore, especially not the diet bit. The world has diets on the brain. I mean, where would the British press be without diets and the Royal Family? It makes me sick.

A girl, maybe twenty, shimmies in from the changing rooms. She doesn't even flinch as she passes the draughts from the emergency doors, although that doesn't irritate me as much as her hair. My heart sinks, it's so strong and healthy. I've seen wigs with healthier looking hair than I've got.

I'm so busy being eaten up by this hair that I don't see Esta McKeever until I'm on top of her.

"Your sonar's not functioning, pet."

"Oh! Sorry, love," I say.

I think a lot about Esta since she became a Born Again. Previous to that, I never had strong feelings about her either way. She was never short of a man when she was a lass and there were those who held that against her. But to me Esta's always been alright. I just never used to think about her like I have since she got God.

I suppose I'd like to believe. I'd like to believe in Father Christmas, too, but I can't anymore. It's hard to remember that far back, but I've a feeling I probably believed in God when I believed in Father Christmas. It was a long time ago.

"Are you stopping or swimming the channel today?" Esta asks.

I give a short laugh and settle with my back to the wall. From my new position, I see Mrs. Weismuller dive in with all the grace of a pantomime cow.

"You're looking well," Esta says.

"I'm not. I look like a transvestite. 'Thou shalt not lie'."

"'Build each other up'."

"Eh?"

"What Paul said."

"Paul who?"

"Paul who yourself. We're having a special charity lunch at church on Sunday. Would you like to come at all?"

"No I would not."

"The idea is Third World food at First World prices and all the money goes to the hungry in Africa."

"Did it ever cross your mind that if God wanted people in Africa to eat better, He'd send them a McDonald's?"

Esta looks at me with patient good humour. She's used to me. "There's enough food in the world for everyone, but God leaves us to sort it out. Free will, you see."

"So God depends on the likes of you to do His work for Him? You'd think He could do better."

"Oh no. It's not a question of ability. It's availability that counts."

"You're like a parrot, you." It really gets me the way she spills out these polished phrases she's picked up at church. "There's no way I could go to your church. I'd need subtitles to understand what they were saying."

Esta laughs and tells me she supposes I'm right. Quite disarming - it's a knack she has.

Jean Mahoney floats up to us. With her red goggles and green and orange cap, she's a sight.

"I'n't it cold?" she says, and I can see that we're trapped here at the deep end.

"I'm sorry about Rover," Esta says.

"Aye, it's all very sad."

"What about Rover?" I ask.

Esta is shaking her head at me.

"Put down," says Jean. "He were hit by the lemonade lorry, a week past on Thursday. It were the kindest thing, really."

"You'll miss him," Esta says.

"Oh, I will."

Some lengths later, Esta floats up to me on her back. She doesn't do backstroke, exactly. She just kicks herself along, lying on her back, no arms, a bit like the Venus de Milo chucked in a pool.

There's a silence. We both sit with our backs to the wall in the shallow end. I nod at Johnny Weismuller and his missus.

"She's like a sea elephant."

Esta says nothing. I've noticed this about her.

"Oh come on. It's not exactly character assassination."

"'The wicked will not inherit the Kingdom of God,' Paul says in Corinthians. 'Neither idolaters, nor thieves, nor slander - "

"Spare me. You Christians are all the same," I tell her. "You think you're the only ones that know owt about goodness. Do you think God's bothered whether or not I make a remark about the Weismullers' diving club?"

"Since you mention it, I think He's bothered about everything."

"Oh well. I wouldn't know as much about Him as you, Esta."

"You could if you wanted to."

"Well, I don't want to." I don't understand how these things get started. It just happens

"I'm sorry you feel that way," Esta says.

And she is - you can tell.

"Don't be," I tell her, and swim off.

As I make my way towards the deep end, I'm feeling more upset than I ought to be. I'm going over and over how God is alright for those that can believe in Him. For the rest of us, He's like a luxury-item: it looks nice in the shop window, but you know you'll never be able to have it for yourself. And I'm angry with Esta for being pleasant when I'm pushing her not to be and for wanting to do what's right.

I'm still thinking about this when I turn for another length and see Johnny Weismuller dive off the side and plunge perfectly into the water. He surfaces and powers towards the middle of the pool. Here Esta is doing her Venus de Milo impression. Johnny reaches her in a few, fluid strokes. I'm wondering what's going on. He stops and stands by her in the water. I keep swimming towards them.

"Oh no!" Johnny shouts in his mahogany voice.

At this, Gordon the attendant springs from his high chair, takes two dancer's steps and dives in, fully clothed.

When I reach Esta, Gordon has pulled up beside her and lowered his feet to the pool floor.

"There's nothing you can do," Johnny tells him. "There's nothing anyone can do."

"What?" I say. I can see Esta, laid out on the water, her eyes stopped still, fixed on the ceiling. I can see a pink flush in them, lots of little pink capillaries, and I think you can't be dead and have bloodshot eyes.

"But she was just - " I say.

"I know," Johnny says. "I know."

I'm thinking he has watched too many people dying in films for his own good and I'm thinking that it's maybe my fault, that I upset her to death. I'm as surprised as he is to find myself whimpering in Johnny Weismuller's arms.

Later, in the showers, I'm stood in the too-hot torrent, which drills into my shoulders. There's a full quota of carcasses in there: me and three others, each standing like a waxwork, silent.

In my mind, I see her floating and wonder how many yards she drifted after she'd gone, how long it was before Johnny made his epic dive. I wonder if Esta's soul left the swimming pool and went straight to God, or was she disappointed at the end?

I go on thinking about it.

PARALLEL WORLDS

Paula Guest

The Beatles crackle from the red-cased wireless on the mantelpiece. *All You Need Is Love.* I want to take my skipping rope outside but Mum glances out of the big window, the one in the living room above the shop front, and says no, it isn't safe. I skip over, without the rope, and looking out I see two men fighting on the corner where Granby and Upper Parliament streets meet. One of them has a knife. It is a sunny day and the rays bounce off the blade and momentarily dazzle me.

After that I don't ask to play outside. As usual, Mum takes us to school, dancing, swimming, the Bookworm Club. At home, the walls of house and family act like the jacket around an immersion heater, keeping in warmth yet impenetrable as a steel vest. The knife is from a parallel world.

Next door to us is the Cariba Club. At weekends the rhythm of steel drums permeates the thick layers of brick and the space between the two buildings. Leroy's mother goes to the club on Saturday nights.

Leroy is always top of the class. He can compute sums in his head that the rest of us can't do with pencil, paper and Miss Bristow. I am always one place behind. I never dream of beating Leroy, but I want to catch up with him in English. Time and again, just as my marks approach his, he slips smartly out of reach.

You would think it is deliberate, a game of cat and mouse, except that Leroy appears to be unaware of it. He is popular with everyone but has no particular friends. His wit and sparkle are magnetic, but rarely can any of us draw his attention.

I am desperate to be his friend. It is odd, because I'm one of the popular children, but I would give up everything to be Leroy's special friend. None of the usual methods work. You can't catch Leroy with sweets and games, party invitations, small acts of kindness.

"What is it you want?" he asks, when offered anything. Or, "Thank you," if it happens to be something he wants, the words and gaze so direct that you know that is the end of it.

Once I had some comics sent by an aunt in California, cartoons of Peewee and Herman, dull colours and matte paper. I prefer my own story papers and their exciting adventure tales of girls in boarding schools and orphanages. I spend all my pocket money on them. I have so many my mother encourages me to bundle them up and sell them and, with the proceeds, I buy fruit for the unfortunate inmates of the nearby children's hospital. I roll the American comics up with my own and take them to school. Leroy, who usually has no interest in the comic sale, comes over to appraise the new material.

"Can I have one?"

"Yes, 2d please," I say.

"I haven't got 2d. Just give me one."

I hesitate.

"Why not?" He fires the words.

"I didn't say no. I'm thinking."

"You don't want them."

"I'm getting fruit for the sick children with the money."

"I only want one."

"But if I give you one I won't be able to sell the rest."

"Why not?"

"Because I can't charge the others if I don't charge you."

"Yes you can. They can afford it."

"But it wouldn't be fair to them."

"You would be fair to me." Leroy always does this, makes everything intensely personal.

A customer, one with cash, comes along and by the time I've given her change and looked up again Leroy has gone.

I put aside a bundle, one with only American comics in it. When the bell goes I take my place behind Leroy in the alphabetical line.

"Leroy," I say. "Here's the comics."

He doesn't turn around, the back of his neck stiff as a starched collar.

"I don't want them," he says.

I try to force the bundle into his hand. "I want to give them to you."

Slowly, he turns his head, eyes glowing like bits of coal in a fire, the look in them old like my granddad's.

"I don't want to have the things you decide you don't want," he says.

I push the comics at him but he makes no attempt to take them and they fall into a puddle, Peewee and Herman trampled into the ground under the feet marching into class.

Not long after that we move from Toxteth. The new house is small and modern, one of hundreds planted by the council like rows of cabbages. There is a shiny black floor, good for clean, sharp strokes from the metal plate on the toe of my tap shoes, but now the nearest dancing class is two buses away.

On my first day in the new school the teacher asks me if I can read.

"Of course I can."

"Which Ladybird book are you on?"

Instantly I am as humble as I have been haughty. I have never heard of Ladybird books. Mrs Davies sends another child to a wire rack in the corner for book 6C. Mrs Davies wears a red woolly polo-neck sweater and sits children in her lap. I think of Miss Bristow, her prickly tweed suit, poker-straight back, steel jaw. You would not be invited to sit on Miss Bristow's knee.

"You open it on the first page, deary, and let me hear what you can do."

The letters are in huge round print, baby writing. Every person in Miss Bristow's class, even those at the bottom, would be able to read this. Mrs Davies mistakes my wounded silence.

"Too difficult?" she asks sympathetically.

"This is a baby's book," I say, all eight-year-old dignity. "I read library books."

She sends my classmate back for 12C, the most advanced in the Ladybird series. I could have read it before I started school and I tell her so.

The sympathy curdles. "Oh dear, a bit above ourselves, aren't we?" she says.

I wonder what Leroy would make of her.

I don't see Leroy again for years, until a couple of days after the riots. I am a cub reporter on the weekly freesheet and Leroy is a poet, a local hero. He is etching words on pavement stones with coloured chalks. The shape of him, still with his starched neck, is unmistakable.

"Leroy." I am as pleased to see him as I had been when a child. "Remember?"

He is crouched over a broken stone, the title of the work in progress "Roast Pork." He doesn't look up.

"Yeah, white bitch. One fucking place behind me."

His hair is in dreadlocks and his words are heavy with Jamaica. At school he used to speak broad Scouse.

"Don't give me that crap. I was a kid round here."

"Yeah." He carries on printing out his free verse, the pace measured, controlled.

"I hardly had a silver spoon in my mouth," I say.

He puts down the pink chalk and moves slowly from crouching to sitting. When he looks up I am startled by the blood in the whites of his eyes, flames licking at the coals.

He nods in the direction of the river. "My great-great-great-grandfather got off a boat down there. Not far up the road, are we?"

"Don't pretend things were better for me," I say, but as the words come out blood rises and stains the skin of my face.

Leroy engages eye contact and sneers. A tide of confusion crashes over me. I feel as I always feel in Leroy's presence - unconfident, on shaky ground, naïve. I want to take the words back, swallow them from the air where they hang between us, defining our separateness.

"I want to understand," I say.

"You already got the answers."

"I tried to give you the bloody comics."

"I remember."

I feel the years evaporate. We are back in the playground.

"You didn't understand. I wasn't disagreeing with you, it just took me longer to follow the argument."

"You still don't get it."

The air is thick with the charred smell of fire.

I tell him: "It's not as simple as you being black and me being white."

"Out of all the kids on this street, not one goes to the university. It's a mile away."

Anger burns me inside, as intense as a child's response.

"No-one else in my street went either."

"You did. I did not."

"I'm proof you can beat the system, Leroy."

"No. No, you're the exception that proves I can't."

"You can't give up."

"You can't run away."

"I always wanted to catch up with you. I wanted us to be friends."

He laughs, a harsh, grating sound. "'Have no friends not equal to yourself.' Confucius, sixth century BC."

"We are equal if we think we are."

Leroy's glare is cold. "You have never thought we are. Difference is, now you don't know who's on top."

It's a funny thing, memory. You give it a stir and you can't tell what will float to the top. I can almost hear the alarm going off in the shop downstairs for the umpteenth time and my mum telling me to stay in bed but getting out anyway and looking out of the window, seeing the smashed glass all over the floor. And later, when the adults come back, I hear Mum saying she saw the policeman stuffing the watches from the tray in the window display into his pockets. And when she asked him about it he said "What's it to you, the insurance'll cover it."

Two days later Leroy is wearing one of the watches. I tell him they're two pounds in our shop and he says he got it from his mum for his birthday and she got it for two-and-six from some man she knows. And when the watches were in the window, all glittery and shiny, I wanted one and was saving my pocket money for it. But when I saw it on Leroy's wrist the shine had gone off it, and I didn't want it any more.

Today I almost see Leroy again. By the time I get here with the camera crew all that's left is the chalk outline the police drew around his body. A car pauses, a cover version of an old Beatles song blaring from it even though the blackened windows are up. There's a thudding drumbeat. If you don't know the words you won't be able to tell what the lyric is. *We Can Work It Out.*

A lone constable keeps back the little knot of people who remain. "Any ideas?" I ask. He shrugs.

The shape of Leroy is on the corner where Granby and Upper Parliament streets meet, where he fell after the knife went in. It looks like one of those cardboard cut-out dolls you used to get in comics years ago, for dressing up with paper clothes.

I look across the road to where our house was before the Compulsory Purchase Order. It is a sunny day and I am momentarily dazzled.

SANDPAPER

Jake Webb

He reached the part of the road that dipped down before rising up again and into the woods and he started counting. The rule had been made when they discovered you could see the other from the door of the house. She would be at the door now and would have just watched him disappear below the dip in the road. Counting softly on her breath, each number a whisper.

"One. Two. Three."

The other rule was that you couldn't miss a number. You had to count at the pace they had agreed, leaving a slight gap between each one. It made sure no one could cheat. Of course there was no real way of enforcing this latest rule. Sometimes he suspected she would leave out numbers, that she started out to the edges of the hiding area before he reached a hundred, but then he stopped himself, saying he had to trust her. They had to trust each other. She drank her tea, continuing the counting in her head while taking sips and swallowing. Despite the cold she had to blow over the rim of the cup, watching the steam give way to the white clouds of her breath. When she was on ninety there was still a little of the browny liquid left, cooled now, and she quickly drank it off, setting the cup down in the snow, into which the last of the heat would almost instantly disperse.

"A hundred," she said, trotting out onto the road and setting off.

He passed the church on seventy. It was called Winterland Chapel and they thought it was abandoned, had been since the end of the war. When the last bell ringer fell to the fever it was quieted for good. The church began to crumble as the bells stiffened with rust. Tiles fell off the roof like scabs and there was no money to replace them. Finally the rafters rotted through and the roof collapsed in a shower of stone and splinters, a flurry of indignant crows cawing off into the sky.

As he jogged past, the priest set out letters on his felt board displaying the following evening's service.

"Good afternoon, young Ben!" he called out.

He knew it was rude but he had to ignore the priest. He picked up his pace even though that was against the rules too. When he reached the outskirts of the woods he stopped counting and turned back towards the house. He knew he didn't have long. He glanced around, hearing his rasps of breath and feeling the red flush on his cheeks. Watery snot was building up in his nostrils already and he felt in his pocket for a tissue. There wasn't one, so he leaned forward and held the pad of a thumb against one nostril and blew snot out of the other.

She passed the church just as he was crawling into his hiding place. The priest was still there, just reaching the dates.

December 2nd;
Evening. Service 7p.m.
All welcome.

She glanced at the lettering. *All welcome.* Stupid, she thought, all the people in the village knew they were welcome. It was what Orla would call a formality, she thought, wondering how formality was spelt.

The priest called out to her; "Young Anna!"

"Hello Father," she said swearing in her head. It was putting the whole thing out of time.

"Your young friend just passed here," the priest told her. "I must say, he seemed in a hurry. He didn't even stop and say hello!"

"Well we're playing a game, Father."

"Oh," he said and looked surprised.

"Hide and seek- you know?"

"Oh," he said again.

"See you," she said starting off again.

"Give your mother my regards!" he shouted after her.

She started trying to work out how much time was wasted speaking to him. He was nice, she thought, but always seemed so nervous. A grown-up, frightened of her!

She reached the woods and looked for footprints first. As usual he had done a good job: several sets of tracks led off in different directions, some coming to an end after a few paces, some doubling back to rejoin the path, some leading off into the woods. She looked closer and saw that some couldn't have been his. There were grown-ups' footprints here, one with a dog's following beside it. She looked at the dog's tracks for a while. Like the pictures of old languages in books at school. She pulled out the top of her jumper from around her neck and let it snap back into place, feeling the sudden pierce of cold then the slow return of warmth.

He crouched inside the log that lay to the left of the path. The numb spread in his legs was already starting but he didn't move. He listened for her feet squeaking in the snow. He tried to decide which would be worse- damp and cold bum, or that tight cramp around his knees. Shifting, he thought, might make too much noise and give him away, so he opted for the second.

In there, the top of his hat just brushed against the soggy roof of the log, every sensation was magnified, every noise from outside amplified. He heard twigs crackling together in the snow and held his breath. A hedgehog looking for a saucer of milk. He heard the low rustle of leaves. Robins looking for berries, or-

"Cheat!"

He sighed. He leaned forward, shifting his weight onto his hands, and crawled along the floor of the log and out into the woods. She was stood waiting for him, her hands on her hips, breathing heavily.

"Cheat!" she repeated.

Awkwardly he brought himself up and wiped snow off his hands.

"You're not allowed to hide in the same place. It's against the rules," she said.

"It's a good hiding place."

"I know it is, but it's not fair! You have to go and hide again."

"Did you spend long looking for me?"

"It doesn't matter. It doesn't count."

He kicked at some snow with his foot.

"Well go on then!" she shouted, turning and closing her eyes and starting to count. He crept round to face her. She had brought up her hands to cover her eyes as if not trusting herself to creep one eyelid open and watch the direction he took. He looked at the colour of her hair, thinking he hadn't really paid much attention to that detail of hers before. "Funny," he thought, "I share a room with her and I haven't ever noticed that." He thought it was the same colour of the trees all around them. He looked to the tops of those trees, the canopy of the woods broken up and cracked under the white sky.

He had forgotten to start counting. He crouched down and, after sifting through the snow, found some bits of broken branches. Moving backwards, away from her, he threw some of them in random directions, listening for the noises they made as they fell back into the snow. He ran several loose circles around her, then started to run in the other direction, jumped up onto the log, ran along the top of it, and at the end took a leap off, landing just where the trees started to get thicker, and without breaking the movement ran off towards the river.

She stopped counting and took her hands away, opening her eyes at the same time. She looked around her. It had started to snow again, and although the scribbles of footprints around them had not yet been completely covered, it was impossible to tell which way he had gone. There were too many sets of tracks going off in too many directions.

While she stood trying to decide which way to start looking she thought how she hadn't heard the snow falling, had only noticed it once she had opened her eyes. She listened carefully now but the smudges of flakes made no sound as they fell, were silent as they piled up in layers. She looked down and imagined they were sheets of paper that she could peel back, one by one, eventually revealing the frozen flowers hidden in the last few sheets.

When he could see the river ahead he started to slow, and when his run became a walk, he took a few paces before turning and looking back. Here the woods began to thin, the spaces between the trees growing wider. If she had chosen the right direction they would easily see each other. He jogged carefully down to the river.

It was freezing. He had only really just noticed. Like sometimes he would look at the sky and think, "It's blue!" as if seeing it for the first time.

As the woods turned dim and grey she realised it was that time, the half-lit hour or so between day and night. She heard noise out on the road; the postman. She ran through the thick snow to meet him. He was whistling a disconnected tune, the notes coming three or four at a time before a pause as he searched for the next ones or started again altogether. The collar of his shiny red coat was turned up and zipped all the way to his chin. She started to giggle. His head didn't look right; it seemed awkwardly perched on top of the collar. She saw his cheeks brushing against it as he turned his head.

"Anna. What you doing out here?"

"Have you seen my brother?"

He stopped, adjusted the strap of his bag. "No. No I haven't. Why - you lost him?"

"Well I'm meant to. We're playing hide and seek. And I can't find him."

The postman winked. "I'd say he's won the game then, hey?" But then his jovial look dropped and he said, "It's cold out here, you know. You sure you ought to be playing?"

"Oh we're fine," she said.

"Tell you what," he said. "I've got to go down to the village so what I'll do is, I'll call in on your mother and see what she says. If you still can't find him come on home and we'll come out and help."

"Okay."

"Okay? See you later then," he nodded, smiling, and set off again. She watched him for a few moments. Down the road the snow-shovellers would be out, she thought, that random committee of people from the village who had to go out and clear the roads. The postman would probably bump into them. But there was nothing particularly interesting about that, she thought.

It was against the rules to go over the river- there had to be a line to mark the boundaries of the game, and that line of black water snaking in and around the forest worked as if someone had put it there solely for them. But, he thought, there was no rule that you couldn't use the river itself. Obviously hiding in the river was out, but what about the space under the bridge, that dank cave of the bank and bottom of the bridge?

He turned back, pleased that he'd discovered a new hiding place so easily, and looked up at the woods. He was half-expecting to see her dot of red coat coming out from the trees on the horizon.

Her red coat. He looked down at his own. Dark blue. "It must," he thought, "be easier to see her than it is to see me. If I was standing between some trees you wouldn't even notice, especially if I had my hood up."

He wandered onto the wet, snowy planks of the bridge. He ran his boot along one. He remembered Orla had been talking recently about how the council was planning to cover all the bridges in the area with sandpaper to make them less slippery, but apparently couldn't seem to find the money.

"That's stupid," he thought. "How much does sandpaper cost?"

She swore, even though she wasn't allowed to. She had heard Orla saying it all the time.

"Shit!"

She couldn't find him. She walked back onto the road to find she was only a short distance from where she had met the postman. He had probably, she thought, delivered most of his letters by now. She stood wondering what to do. It was times like this that Orla always lit a cigarette.

"Maybe I should start smoking," she thought.

She started walking back down the road to the village.

He was stood leaning over the rail of the bridge spitting into the water. When the little gob of spit landed he ran across the bridge to the other side to watch it appear on the other side and float happily downstream, but either the water was running too fast or he wasn't running fast enough; each time the spit was nowhere in sight. After five or six tries he started to run out of spit. He rubbed his tongue against the sides of his mouth, trying to coax more out. On the seventh try he turned and ran as soon as he let the spit go. It was just as the thought came that perhaps the spit dissolved in the river water while going under the bridge- aha!- that he slipped, his feet losing their grip and arching up from beneath him. He flailed, trying to regain some sort of balance. It was the back of his head that hit the bridge first.

When she got back to the house it was snowing again and her feet were burning-cold from walking in the snow that had already fallen. The snow that had been there for- she couldn't think. It was always there. She started thinking of the layers again, wondering; if snow fell every day, why wasn't it piled up around the tops of the trees?

In the kitchen the postman and Orla sat opposite each other at the table drinking tea and talking importantly. When Orla saw her she stood up angrily.

"There you are!"

"Hi."

"Where's Ben?"

"I don't know."

Orla shot a hasty look at the postman who immediately swallowed the last of his tea and stood up pulling his coat on.

"You mean you haven't found him?"

"No. Is he not here?"

"No he's not." Orla started tapping the table quickly which she only did when she was worried.

The postman zipped his coat up and leaned to look out of the window. Big lazy flakes screening behind the glass. "I'll just go and round up the boys, Orla," he said.

"They'll probably be out on the junction shovelling," she said following him through to the door.

"Fine. You going to wait here?"

She couldn't hear what they were saying after that. She heard the door closing. She looked through the glass to the country outside where it was getting dark. When she turned round Orla was standing there looking at her.

"Well?" Orla said.

"He will be all right won't he?"

"Let's hope so."

She started to cry. "I don't want Ben to die!"

Orla softened and came over. "There. He won't die. Sjogren and the others are out there now, they'll find him."

"He won't be far away, cause, cause, we've got this rule where..."

"There..."

"...where you can't go outside the river..."

She cried. And he had won again, she thought.

She went to their room. She wasn't sent there as punishment, she wanted to go there and look at his things. She looked at his picture-books on the little shelf and his yellow bear with the purple ribbon round its neck on the top bunk-bed. That made her think of the time he wet himself during the night and she was woken up by his shouting then the warm smelly liquid dripping through the mattress above her head.

"Why did you wee yourself anyway?" she said.

"I had a scary dream."

"What about?"

"A silly dog."

She started to giggle now and thought, "I shouldn't laugh! I shouldn't laugh!"

She went to the small window that looked out over the fields and the rest of the village. She saw the hall where they went on the first night of the Festival. She saw the shapes of the stars. She saw the snow.

He was thinking of pebbles when they found him. Pebbles clicking against each other, rattling, echoing, smoothed by millions of years of water.

It was cold and black and white. He tried to lift his head but couldn't. He saw the lights first, then heard the voices, the calls sounding out and carrying to the bridge. Men approaching with those lights. Beams swinging out of the woods towards him.

She didn't see what was happening but she heard from their room at the top of the stairs. She was lying on the bed. "How could I have fallen asleep when he was out there freezing!" she thought.

The noise of sudden activity in the house.

"Get him in, quick!"

"Get him through to the kitchen."

"Orla!"

The door slammed shut behind the men. She listened but couldn't tell how many there were. They were all talking at once in the same low grown-up voice.

"God above!" she heard Orla shouting.

"He'll be all right. Get some hot water going."

"And blankets."

"We need to get him out of these wet clothes."

She sat on the edge of the bed listening, her feet twitching, not sure whether to go down and help. They would only tell her to go back to her room. She would say, "Is he all right?" and she would be bustled out. "We don't know, you'll just have to wait."

Footsteps padded quickly past the door to the cupboard at the end of the hall. The door opened and she knew Orla would be pulling out blankets. She listened to the heater humming in the corner of the room. She sprang up off the bed and ran to the door. She paused after putting her hand on the knob. They would only tell her to go back upstairs.

"Why are we always only in the way!" she shouted to herself.

The warmth came back the same way as the cold had come. Slowly spreading into him. All the rings on the cooker were burning- that was the first thing he saw, the warm blue flames burning quietly as if Orla was just about to cook soup. The potatoes thumping together in the sink as she washed them.

"I feel horrible," he said looking around at Orla and all the men peering at him anxiously. They all laughed.

More happened. She sat on the floor by the heater first bouncing his yellow bear up and down on her knee then looking at her book of maps. The pastel yellows and blues, the random jagged roads like lines on a palm, the distorted concentric circles like ripples on a pond. Those are the mountains below here, she thought. She looked at the cities, the huge blocks of colour broken-up where roads went through. The door opened and it was only then she realised all had gone quiet in the house. The men must have gone. Orla was leading him in gently. His hair was all mussed up and he had a blanket wrapped round him.

"Ben!" She jumped up and hugged him.

"Hi."

"Are you okay?"

"I'm still cold."

"You need to go to bed," Orla said. She wasn't angry anymore. She was too relieved to be angry. "In fact," she added, "you both ought to be off."

"I'm not tired though Orla!"

"But Ben is."

"Only a little," he said.

"A little's enough."

Orla had to lift him into the top bunk. He couldn't climb the ladder.

"You too Anna!"

"I'm going, I'm going!"

"I'll be back up in a few minutes."

Orla closed the door behind her. She waited until she could hear her footsteps reach the bottom of the stairs before jumping onto the ladder so she could see him.

"Don't ever do that again!" she shouted.

"Sorry."

"I was worried!"

"I know you're not allowed to go past the river. But I was under the bridge on this side- it's kind of allowed isn't it?"

"I didn't mean that, stupid!" she said hugging him again.

THE MEMORY OF WATER

Helen Newall

A fisherman found a seal tangled in his nets, and though the dusk was falling and the tide turning and seals were foragers for his fish, he decided to spare it and he dove into the swell with his knife and cut it free. But the turn of the tide and the moon being full made strange currents in the ocean and the fisherman was swept out to sea. But then, as he was saying his last prayers, there swam alongside him a woman with sleek dark hair who pulled him to the shallows, safe from the ninth wave, and hauled him onto the sands of a little rocky island, whereupon she wrapped her silver pelt about her and slipped back into the water, and all he could see about him was seals bobbing in the silver ocean, singing as the moon rose over.

Stories from the Northern Isles
William Macreadie 1879

My name is Seth and I got washed up on an island. Black rock and the silver fizz of light on the water. It dazzled me. That's what I remember seeing.

There are photographs of who I used to be. Bits of frozen time. In isolation they are nothing, but pasted together, a montage, they are a journey. They can give me bad dreams.

Image One: A Photograph.
Black and white. A beach. A little boy squints into the sun. He stands holding hands with a smiling man. The boy's left hand is

stuffed into the pocket of his shorts because he is clutching a knife. I know this. Moments after the shutter clicks the smiling man finds the knife.

When I was that boy, on a holiday, in a gift shop, I stole a knife, and there was a lot of grief about it. When I was found out my mother wept and held my hand and smoothed down my hair and said it was very, very wrong. And then my father, white with rage, held my hand and talked, fidgeting all the while. I didn't hear the words, I only saw my small white hand in his palm and then he smacked the knuckles sharply with the side of a ruler so that there was a deep red stinging line in the skin that prickled tears into my eyes and choked a lump into my throat. But I wouldn't cry. And nothing hurt as much as the loss of the knife.

But nobody understood. It was a knife. It was stealing. But I didn't steal it for its cutting edge, or the black bone handle, or the thick polished leather sheath. Not for the possession of it. I didn't steal it. It stole me. Possessed me. Drew me into it with its brilliance and an edge so keen that when I tilted the blade to the window it cut the light and reflected it in swift fierce slashes over the walls. It was the light I held silently in a corner of a shop while my mother chose postcards and my father leafed through guide books. It was this light that I slipped into my pocket.

They didn't return the knife to the shop. My father kept it. I know this because many years after, when I went through his things searching secretly for something else, I found it pushed to the back of a drawer. It was a weight my fumbling fingers touched and then grasped, but even then, in that brief moment before I pulled it out into the thin moonlight I swear I could sense the cold magic of the metal. Even through the leather sheath it pulsed some dark message into my hand. Like the memory of electricity. As if an ancient circuit had been reconnected and a cold blue echo tingled in my skin, and I had stolen the light again.

Image Two: A Dream.
A face under water. Vivid blue and green and silent motion. Like old reels of scratched ciné 8 film on a home projector.

I always saw the same distant face in a peculiar underwater landscape, shafts of light spindling through green water. And far above me the sparkling fluid mosaic of the surface. I'm floundering, rolling, my limbs windmilling through the clear suffocating green, but the face is close by. A white face. Smooth and rippled with water light. Why? I scream at the face. Shoals of chrome bubbles tumble up from my mouth. She opens her eyes. I don't know, she says.

Who is drowning here and who rescues who?

Is it possible to take photographs of dreams? I've always had beautiful dreams, even after a beating. Even after long nights long ago lying in a hot tangled bed listening to my dad beat the shit out of my mother. The monotony of pain. Always the same hot agony as I stuff my head under a pillow to muffle out the crying, and as I do I play the film in my head, desperate for something to stop. To be different. Be someone else.

Image Three: A Memory.
It feels like a dream. No colours anymore. There are no photographs now. I'm a ten year old tearaway, circling the streets on a bike, stealing sweets from the newsagents, breaking windows with bits of brick. It's always raining in these memories, and I've no coat. And there are stray dogs and wet newspapers and grass verges claggy with mud and fag buts, and when I'm brought home in the back of yet another police car my mother can't wait to get rid of

them because she's stone cold sober and as soon as she's closed the door she starts stuffing clothes into suitcases with the curtains drawn and whispering plans to me for our getaway.

How many suitcases does it take to realise it's never going to happen?

When I grew up I was going to be a poet. I grew up waiting for a signal. Aged nine: let's go. Thirteen: let's do it now, while he's out. Fifteen: what are we waiting for? What are you frightened of? I'm not frightened. And she wasn't frightened either because when her hands shook so badly she couldn't hold the door keys she'd have a drink.

"Dutch courage," she'd say. And she'd hold me tightly and we'd sit on the cases behind the front door and she'd drink some more and cry and I'd think about the stories I read of the brave little Dutch boy who saved the day by plugging the crack of a crumbling dike with his finger. And about the fisherman saving the selkie. And then as if she could read my mind...

"Tell me a story," she said.

"What story?"

"Anything. Tell me anything."

But I couldn't tell her those stories. The happy endings always made her cry. Remember my dream? The face in the water? I told her that.

When it got dark she'd fumble with the keys for the keyhole in the front door, her hands shaking even more, and then she'd slam the bolts into their catches. It was a sound that echoed through the house. There is an imprint of its sound wave resonating still in my head; it haunts me when it's dark and I catch the smell of whisky fumes. It's never the ghost of that sound that frightens me. It's what happened next.

We'd huddle upstairs and wait for the hammering to begin. Late evening. No lights on in the house, only the yellow sodium sifting in through the curtains. And then him battering on the door.

She always unlocked it. I'd hide under a bed, or behind a chair, and he'd smash through the unlocked door and kick her. Again and again and again and again and again and...

Afterwards, in the dark, I'd pour her more whisky. I had to hold the glass to her broken mouth. She never let me put the light on. The blood was always dark against her skin. Never fully lit. Never red.

"You're not like him," she'd whisper. "You're not the same." And she'd touch my hair with injured fingers. She said it so many times I didn't hear her anymore until one night when I rinsed out a glass for her in the bathroom and saw my face reflected and thought about his thin fair hair. Then I heard what she said. There was a transformation. It was as if the mirror shattered. As if I saw my dark curling hair and my brown eyes for the first time. But when I asked her about it she said nothing. Shook her head.

That was how it was I went hunting for something, anything to prove we weren't connected. A letter, a paper, a birth certificate. Something that ruptured the bloodline. That was when I found the knife again in the back of his desk drawer.

What pictures did you see when I told you all that?

Did you imagine a council house in a run down bit of town? Thin streets and worn out clothes and blank hopeless faces? Well, smash it and rebuild it. Take another photograph. Our house was set in seven acres of trimmed lawns and bluntly pruned roses. There were gardeners. Nothing must grow wild. No suckers. No weeds. And in the house no dust must fall on the wood and the crystal. There was a daily cleaning lady to see to it all. And all of it was shit. A facade. Like a lath and plaster film set propped up with sticks and stage weights. Let's pretend we're a Happy Family. He wasn't my dad anyway.

Sometimes, he'd pick me up from school in a car with leather seats and a walnut dashboard and we'd ride smoothly home in polish-scented silence. I think I noticed then that he couldn't say my name. It choked him to say it.

"Keep your mucky shoes off the seats, you little bastard."

"My name is Seth."

He wanted to send me away to a school but my mother must have stood her ground on that one. Perhaps that was the first time he hit her. The first time the walnut veneer fell away.

"Why?" I'd say when I was still young enough to ask.

"I don't know," she'd cry in the dark, drinking whisky and the silence of unexplained screaming intensified. Like light slowly dimming through all the rooms in an empty house. No television because it polluted the mind. No radio because it was meaningless noise. No record player because music was best heard live. Lots of books. A universe of books.

The Book of Heroes.

The Wonder Book of Great Scientific Men.

Little Women.

Big dusty blue leather books with gold lettering.

Bedtime Stories for Tiny Girls and Boys.

Books with thick brown mottled pages from some faded childhood, and others from a study of things more dark and mysterious.

The Golden Bough. Print too small.

The Origin of the Species. No pictures.
Inventions and Discoveries in Full Color. The Telephone.
Chilling Tales of Supernatural Horror. The other side.
The Periodic Table. The weight of atoms. Mercury. Hg. Silver. Ag. A transition element.
Modern Electronics. Electricity and water do not mix.
Stories from the Northern Isles. A guide book for my mind. I loved it. I knew every gold edged page of it, and all the pictures in it. And when I fancied a change I read the others. Pored over the colour plates. Examined the diagrams. And they printed silver lines of connection into my brain, building the circuitry of my imagination. Silver. A transition element. Never underestimate my imagination. It's a dangerous thing.

Nine. Thirteen. Fifteen. I got tall. I grew my dark hair long because he was blond and he wore his cut short. Like his lawns. Like his sentences. And when my body matured and he resented the extra space it occupied, he used to refer to me as if I wasn't there. What isn't there can be very powerful. And things change. Observation changes them. I experimented. I split the atom of his silence. I began tapping odd rhythms on the central heating pipes. But like a scientist stumbling over a glowing new element, I found something life changing. Unpredictability. It has many important properties, the most radioactive of which is fear.

One late summer night when I was seventeen, I pulled a knife on him. My twice-stolen knife. Why did I do it? Why then? I did it just to see what it was like and it was fucking excellent.

I waited for him in the dark at the top of the stairs, and as the ritual played itself out, my heart began to pound the blood through me, as if for the first time. As if I was alive for the first time. My mother stood afraid in the darkness. He shouted through the letterbox. She wept and I heard her unlocking the door, and then he came barging in, flinging the door back so hard the glass shattered, and I thundered down the stairs, and leapt across the distance and grabbed at his raised fist with one hand and pointed the knife with the other. She screamed. There was a lot of shouting. Steel flashed. And light on things. That's what I remember. I remember the outside lights burnishing the brilliance of the steel and glittering on the jags of glass in the door. Jesus. The peace of it. Like slow motion. Like holding your breath under water with the pressure roaring in your ears. The chaos didn't touch me at all because I held the knife...

...until I let go of his wrist and he staggered back, almost pulling me over. In the silence my mother crawled slowly away and slumped on the bottom stair.

"Put that down," he said, but I didn't move.

"Why?" I said, but he stared at the knife, hypnotised by the flash of it pointed at him. And the knife scorched my shaking hand and electrified the air. Wild steel white electricity.

"I said put it down," he said softly, slowly, and still I didn't move. Nobody moved. For hours. Weeks. Years. Nobody moved. Till I screamed. Shattering all the silences of so many years.

"Don't fucking tell me what to fucking do, Shit Head." I screamed it and it felt as if my face exploded and I turned the knife under his nose slowly, so slowly, and then I laughed because I could see the sweat prickling on his face and my mother began to cry, and this man who had smiled in all the photographs of us on the beach, smiled and shrank back against the door jamb. And I smiled too.

It was very still. Still enough for a ritual. So I lifted my left hand to where the knife cut the air and slowly, slowly, slowly drew the blade over the skin on the back of my hand. I slit it where the ruler had lined the skin so many years before. The first circuit. The first connection. It didn't hurt. It was easy. It was good. And blood sprang from the line I drew and dribbled through my fingers, warm and dark. In the silence I heard the first droplet drip onto the parquet.

"Say my name," I whispered.

"Seth," my mother said quietly.

"Not you. Him." My step-dad shifted. I pointed the knife at him again so fast a bead of blood flicked from its point and flecked his face.

"I'm calling the police," he croaked, but he couldn't take his eyes from the blade. And neither did my mother.

"Say my name," I said. And he couldn't so I slashed my skin again. He shut his eyes. Another cut.

"Seth," he whispered at last. And I cut again, again and again, up my arm. Red lines that have now turned to silver. Like circuits. Like prophecies written in runes.

My mother could have stopped me. At any time she could have stopped me. Really, she could. All she had to do was ask me to drop the knife and I'd have done it. But she didn't, and this was approval, wasn't it? Because, just like me, she saw the light on the blade and she liked the power of it. My twice-stolen knife. It mesmerised her.

How many centuries pass like this? In all of them, the power was shifted. But what did I do with all this power? How did I wield it? What happens now? I thought. What happens next?

I didn't know, so I backed off, still pointing the knife at his throat, blood lacing my hands and my arms.

"Never. Touch. Her. Again," I hissed, and then I lowered my

arm and walked away.

I heard my mother gasp, and the rush of him gathering himself, flying for me, bellowing as he leapt, and, as he grabbed for my shoulder, I ducked aside and the knife clattered to the floor and spun, and he sprawled heavily on the hall rug and I kicked him hard again and again and again, screaming each time my foot made contact. He wheezily grunted to the rhythm of my kicking, and scrabbled for escape and got nowhere. And it was my mother's turn to cry out and run and hide and scream.

Shit Head. I should have killed you. I should have fucking kicked you to death.

But I didn't. I snatched up my knife and ran through the open door, out into the night where the pools of light from the street lamps were dangerous islands of illumination and the darkness in between was terrifying and far off car tyres swished on wet roads and headlights that approached and sped past were all after me hunting me and the clang of my heels on the midnight pavements rang echoes through the misty drizzle that jarred my head and which everyone must hear and the air was cold as I ran and it cut my lungs and stung in my cut skin and froze the tears that bled down my face till I was breathless and coughing with the ache of it and stabbed with a digging pain in my side like a hot searing knife but I couldn't stop running.

How old was I when I ran? I was seventeen. I was fifteen. I was nine. I was scared and hurting and I didn't go home for three days.

This is me. I am Seth. My skin is a network of silver lines. Like circuits tattooed into me to tell me who I am. I've got photographs to prove who I am.

I crouched for three days in a derelict house and I wanted to phone home. I wanted to phone so badly it ached and I dreamed of water, but it was the light sifting onto my face through the ivy over the window. Strange dreams. Black rocks and silver water and rain dripping in through the rafters above me, splashing me awake. In this half light, a broken mirror above a sink full of wet leaves reflected back his face. So I smashed it and cut my finger and when I saw the blood I cried.

Or perhaps I didn't do that at all. Things can be mad and random. And dreams make the strange familiar and the familiar strange. I don't know what I did. But, whatever I did, I could see the invisible silver line slashed through the air from me to him. Everything is linked. Soldered into time with blood. And in the darkness the silver of the knife was stained. His blood, not mine. I screamed it silently. Pacing the streets. Running through the evening streets. Through the heat wave, sweat dampening my shirt to my body like a bruise. And the lacerations in my skin glowed as if there were fine silver wires embedded in them that bound me to the metal of the knife forever.

And on the third night, all washed up and no-where to go, I found myself standing, breathing heavily, gripping rusted iron railings on a hilltop in a dark bit of city where stunted leafless trees scratched the skies like twists of loose black wires and the grass and the soil and the nettles were slowly swallowing old flagged pavements and a burnt-out car and used needles and broken dolls and I looked out over the city, listening to the distant traffic roar.

The sunset raged above the river, and the cluttered lights were coming on along roads and in tower blocks, flickering in the dusk haze of car fumes. Sirens and radios and neon and blood and iron and blue lights and the smell of damp newspaper and the knife in my hand. They all fused till I had to get out of my head, out of my skin, out of my life before the insanity of it all tangled me up in it forever.

I lay down on the soil and it was damp and cool in the scent of decay and I listened to the city dogs barking and watched a few stars come out and I held the knife in my fist and I stabbed the blade into the earth next to my thigh again and again and again and...

Now, I do not know what happened. Something happened. I smelled silver disturbing the air. An element. Transition. Like another frequency. An oscillation. Tinnitus. Jesus. A sickening resonance. No impedance. The darkness amplified it and I had the memory of water.

> In a flash. Particles of silver coalesced. They made a negative that printed a positive. And I was somewhere else. On a beach. On an island. Someone touched my face. Fingers smoothed my hair. A woman bending over me, her face lost in darkness, hidden in a swinging veil of wet black hair. I smelt the sea, pungent and cold. And heard the white crash of breakers on rocks. Cold inhaled water prickled bronchioles. It was as if my lungs were sparkling. And a memory of a fish shoal silvered the mesh of the dream. Not a dream. This was not a dream. And then she stood and moved away, out of vision, and, when I sat up to watch her go back into the ocean, she was no-where. The beach was empty. The particles dissolved.
> White noise.

The wind blew. The moon rose. A scrap of paper rolled. Distant traffic. Sirens. Dogs barked. Darkness fell and the city lights blazed and stained the night sky orange and her touch still tingled on my skin. Like wetness in a breath of wind. Like the memory of water. But I was alone, shivering, the knife still heavy in my hand, its blade smeared with wet soil as dark as my mother's blood, and everything was the same. And everything was different.

So now you want me to tell you I rescued her. That I went back and cut him out of our lives forever. No such transformation. I didn't need to. Some little punk did it for me. I can imagine it. The boy trashing a phone box, beating up the walls, kicking out the glass from the red frames because he can't get a connection, kicking everything, punching everything till his hands bleed and his forehead is studded with shards of glass and there are grits of glass glittering on the wet pavement. And this is what my dad walks into. He's looking for me. His son. And this is what he finds and, good citizen that he is, he steps in and shouts at the little bastard to stop it.

And the little bastard stops it and stabs him. The violence of strangers is an incomprehensible thing. I find their compassion even stranger. The little bastard phoned for an ambulance. I can see it all. But before the sirens came blaring into the street, my dad bled to death on a summer evening, on a bier of broken glass and it wasn't yet dark enough to hide the red of the blood that soaked his shirt. And there wasn't a reliable witness to tell of the shadow who fled into the dusk like something swimming just below the surface of the sea.

Or perhaps I didn't do that at all. Things can be mad and random.

I AM A BOBBIE PERU

Robert Doyle

I always loved motorcycles and so it was natural that as soon as I could get out of school I'd go to work with bikes, fixing them and then racing them in motor-cross and later on at the speedway. My dad and me mates were happy when I was fixing bikes but when it come to racing them they sort of looked at me and asked me, -well, this was my dad really - what the hell was I doing with my life. Me dad thought I was a nutter and a dead beat. He said I was a dreamer, and dole fodder, and wanted to know why I turned me nose up at going in with me mate to start a business selling car batteries. I tried to tell him I wanted to be more than that, that I wanted to be famous. But he just looked at me and said I couldn't stop at home for much longer and that I needed to get me head screwed on.

Me dad went up the wall when I told him I was going to be a stunt bike rider, he was worried about me getting myself killed and what sort of a trade was it for a man when me and Debbie, me girlfriend, had a baby on the way. My mum wanted to know why I was doing it and I said to her "I'm a Bobbie Peru, whatever that is." She nodded her head but you could tell she didn't understand.

After a while me dad came round and he was just magic. He helped me get my bike ready; he'd been a big fan of bikes when he was a kid an all and I suppose he was either proud of what I was doing or jealous - but not in a bad way - or he just wanted a hobby or something. Soon after moaning about a bit and drinking every last drop of tea in the garage, he was working with me on little jumps, getting the angles right and even bringing one of his mates from the pub who used to be a maths teacher to help get the angles right.

We got things just about right on small jumps and I was all for going for something bigger but me dad put me straight on that right away and his mate said the same.

Me dad said: " What if you break your bloody neck and no-one's around to see it? If you're going to do yourself in you may as well get paid."

And me dad was right.

We went to see Steve who's the manager of the speedway track and put the idea to him that between races I'd do some jumps in the middle. He thought it was a brilliant idea, didn't know why he hadn't thought of it before, and he started stretching his arms out with his palms up like Moses and starts saying, "See the daredevil death-defying, amazing Rock Tiger and his motorcycle thrill show."

I put him straight on that straight away, I said: "All that other stuff's okay but me name is Bobbie Peru, that's what goes on the poster," and he shrugged and said: "Okay, mate, whatever you want."

Then he asked me how long I'd been doing jumps and I was about to tell him but me dad coughed in and said: "About 10 years, mostly in France."

Steve was dead impressed with this, you could tell, especially the French bit, and me dad saw it and started getting him into it even more by going on about how we all got our fair share of French birds, me him and 'The Professor' as he had stated calling his mate, and how they was all gagging for it over there because we were a bit of rough trade. And by now Steve is on the edge of his seat, egging me dad on to give him some descriptions and me dad is going, "Well, there was this one girl - and I'm sitting back in my chair watching me dad while he's making up all this stuff and me dad is loving it. I mean, really loving every second of it, like he really was in France, like he really did have all these sexy French birds and had all these adventures. I think my dad is having his early years all over again, through me and the bikes and the show. It's like he regrets getting married and having me and our Laura and Jenny and working on at the Spam factory instead of going on one of them round the world back-packing cruises or something.

Steve asks why we came back from France and me dad says it's because of them EEC bastards who, and you won't believe this, mate, come up with a rule that you've got to be a French citizen to get a permit to ride on a motorbike. Steve tuts and then he shakes his head and looks to an empty chair as if it's got someone in it then he leans on the table and his voice drops and he says:

"Typical that is, they burn all our fucking sheep and we keep shelling out for their bloody farmers and they're all coming over here, like, but then when we go over there it's just: oh no me-sure. Just because we're English and they hate the English, even when it was us that saved them in the war and all that."

He stops and me and me dad know that me dad's made a bit of a mistake. He's gone too far.

"Do youse need one of them permits over here, I mean what about insurance and the council and that?" Steve asks.

"Nah," says me dad and The Professor joins in to make it sound even better and says, "Do we fuck" in a long, drawn out way.

"The bloody Krauts haven't taken us over yet. We just write you a letter saying that if anything goes wrong then it's no blame on you, that we was the ones who wanted to do it. No-one can stop you jumping if you want to do it; it's a free country."

"I don't know," says Steve and he's moving about in his chair like he's got something up his arse.

"I get loads of hassle over the bloody noise as it is - the buggers knew they was moving in next to a bloody track when they moved here - I don't want to make it worse. It's only twice a week and they never stop fucking moaning."

Then me dad works his old magic, the phrase that he uses everytime to get what he wants, I've seen it in action hundreds of times and it's never failed yet. My dad goes, "Oh, right, well, if you want to go back on your word ..."

He always lets his voice trail off a bit at the end and Steve, like all the rest before him, shoves out his hand and says:

"Oh no, I'm not saying that, it's just, well, you know..."

My dad interrupts and says:

"No, that's okay. I mean, my word is my bond, but if you want to go back on your word then there's nothing we can do."

And he adds, for good measure, "Isn't that right, Professor?"

And The Professor says, "There's not a damn thing we can do about it."

Bingo. Steve waves his hand like he's getting rid of a wasp in his sleep.

"Okay, okay. We'll do it but I want that letter before anyone jumps over anything, all right?"

"You bet," says my dad with a little smile on his face. And everyone shakes hands and we leave the little office and head for the pub to celebrate, with my dad slapping The Professor on the back and whooping it up with me buying the first round.

I'd always been a big fan of Evel Knievel and when I was a kid I had a little of model of him that sat on a bike that you put in this red machine with a big handle that you'd whazz around and around until your arm was nearly going to break off and then the bike would shoot out and go flying down the room and I always had some annuals propped up on tins of beans or something and the bike would whazz right up and go flying through the air. It was brilliant. Really boss. I remember one time getting a load of kids in the street to lie down on the floor so I could jump my Evil Knievel over them over a really big ramp and so I'm whazzing it away and it goes and makes the perfect take off but just doesn't quite make it and it hits some girl, the last in the line, on the head and the back wheel whazzer gets all caught up in her hair and no matter how hard we pulled we just couldn't get it out and she went legging off home to her dad to get it cut out and her dad come round to the house and started having a go at my dad and in the end me dad had to give him a slap to get rid of him. Me dad gave me a bloody good hiding that night. He said he'd make sure that I couldn't sit down for a week and he was almost right. He battered me, really battered me, and he slung out me Evil Knievel bike and that was worse than getting slapped. But I remember thinking at the time that even though he'd slung out the bike and I couldn't play with it any more I still had the whazzer machine and the Evil Knievel actual figure and the box. I liked the box best of all; it was real America. I used to stare at the box for hours on end and read the Evil Knievel story that come with the instructions and for hours I'd just dream about meeting Evil Knievel and how we'd be really good mates and how he'd help me become a stuntman and look after me and buy me a bike and call me "The Kid".

"How's it going, Kid?" Asks me dad. "Feeling okay?"

We're back in Steve's office, waiting for a gap in the speedway action to do our turn. The roar of the bikes is making my heart beat faster and I'm glad I just had a nibble of toast for breakfast otherwise I'd be calling for Hughie for sure. The Professor is out with some of the speedway blokes setting up the ramps now, it's not far off. And like I'm really nervous.

The show almost didn't come off at all. I came up with the idea of jumping over a cage full of dogs, because Evil Knievel's first jump was over a cage with a mountain lion in it and a wooden crate filled with snakes. The Professor was all for it, and eventually we talked my dad into the idea, but then the RSPCA heard about it. Well, The Professor gets down there and asks if he can borrow some dogs from them, and they came down and threatened to get Steve arrested if any animals were used in the stunt. Steve rang us up saying that everything was off, that this is just the hassle he didn't need. Luckily me dad worked his old "you're not going back on your word" trick and the show was back on the road. The whole thing pissed off The Professor, though.

"I just can't work it out," he said. "I didn't want the main bloody dogs, just the ones they was going to put to sleep. I said we'd even keep a few of them for the show if things worked out: but no, they'd rather gas the poor buggers. You should of seen this jumped up little Hitler, Bobbie. Looking down his bloody nose, saying 'putting any animal in a cage and jumping a noisy motorcycle over it will cause massive distress'. I'll tell you what I near flipped. I tell you what, if them dogs could talk they'd take the show any day of the fucking week than go to them bloody gas chambers. It's criminal what they do to them dogs. Just criminal."

We decided on pouring a load of petrol on the grass and lighting it and then me jumping over it. The Professor said I'd be going so fast and there'd be so much wind that the flames wouldn't get me or the bike. I trusted him, even though I'd found out the other day that he wasn't ever really a maths teacher but he worked in the bookies and doing maths problems was just his hobby.

I got out onto the track and they started playing this really ace music; duh, duh, duh, duh - du-duh. The fella on the mike was really giving it loads and the punters were cheering. I got on me bike and me dad put me helmet on, I gave him a smile and he gave me a wink. The Professor gave me a thumbs up sign. First I rode some wheelies, really getting a load of noise out of the bike and spraying up a load of dirt from the track. The crowd really liked that and I could hear them cheering so I did some extra-super wheelies. This was the best laugh I had ever had and I'm giggling away like mad to myself.

Finally it comes time to do the jump. Me dad and The Professor pour petrol all over the space between the two ramps - we'd made the ramps ourselves with big long, smoothed down planks of wood, and painted them red white and blue like on the Evil Knievel box - and the crowd give one last cheer and then they go all quiet. I get a good distance and accelerate towards the ramp, upshifting through the gears, keeping my eye on the ramp that's coming closer and closer and closer.

Thump!

The bike hits the ramp and up the ramp I go.

Whazz!

Right into the sky. There's a second of pure joy and then I see the landing ramp, I see that baby coming closer and I grit my teeth, and ohhhhhh Shit.

Boom!

I'm alive. I've landed. I speed down the end of the ramp.

Bam!

The front wheel hits the dirt and I nearly go over the handle bars but I grit my teeth. Oh, God.

Bam!

The back wheel hits the dirt and I'm all over the place but I stay on and I'm not on fire and the crowd cheer and I skid the bike to a stop and me dad and The Professor are running towards me and I pull off my helmet and wave it at the crowd and they're just going nuts. Me dad is slapping me on the back and he's shivering all over and crying.

"Perfect, son. Bloody perfect, son," he says.

A load of people have come out of the crowd and are slapping me on the back and grown men are introducing me to their sons. This is really it. A lad gives me a programme to sign and I almost sign it Evel Knievel but I remember who I am and I sign it Best wishes, Bobbie Peru. The kid clutches the autograph and says:

"That was brilliant, that was really brilliant."

And I say:

"That's okay, Kid. Remember to always do your homework."

And I'm thinking because he made me feel like one, this kid is the real star.

TODAY WE HAVE NAMING OF POEMS

Carol Smith

Mr Banner sighed as he looked up and down the aisles. Fifteen-year-olds, the boys as big as men and the girls as much trouble as their mothers had been before them. Poetry. It might as well be Swahili for all the interest they took. He'd wrestled them through from 12 year-olds doing *Cargoes* to this, finishing the American Poets. Not one of them would ever read a poem again. He decided, suddenly, to read *Cargoes* to them, to see if three years had matured their thought processes in any way. His voice lifted when he got to *Dirty British coaster with it's salt-caked smoke stack, butting through the Channel in the mad March days.* He stressed *butting* and *Channel* and *mad March*.

Maureen liked this bit best, better than *Quinquireme of Ninevah*, because she didn't know what that meant and she had never seen a peacock or any of the other fancy things. There was a toughness, she thought, in the dirty British coaster - out there doing its job - fighting the mad March days. The sea would be high in March, whipped up by winds, up over the sides of the ship, huge waves and walls of water rushing by. The sea around sunny Palestine wouldn't be like that at all. *Cargoes*, she liked that word - *cargoes* - it sounded lovely when she said it to herself.

'Well?' Mr Banner said. 'Comments?'

No-one spoke.

'Have you nothing to say? Were you not moved at all by this? Have you all been struck dumb by the eloquence of my rendition?'

Maureen knew enough to keep her mouth shut. Mr Banner laid traps for the unwary.

'Sir?' Ian Dempsey put his hand up. 'Sir, I don't think it's fair to compare things like that and for Britain to look worse than other places.'

Mr Banner had his 'God Almighty' face on. 'Is that a fact?' he said. 'Three years I've had you lot. You've garbled your way through grammar and stuttered your way through Shakespeare. I couldn't be more pleased that this is your last day! Let's get on and finish the Americans. Archibald McLeish. Born in Glencoe, Illinois, he moved to France in 1923 to begin his career as a writer. In 1932 he won the Pulitzer prize for his poem *Conquistador*. The poem I'm going to read is called *Ars Poetica*.'

Maureen heard a whisper behind her, 'It says *arse* in the book!'

There was a flurry of giggles. Mr Banner looked stern. 'Archibald McLeish was appointed as Librarian of Congress, he was Boydston Professor of..."

Maureen drifted off, into the poem.

A poem should be palpable and mute as a globed fruit, she read. *Dumb as old medallions to the thumb.*

She could feel the medallions. They had been traced by fingers for centuries and now they were smooth. Warm and smooth. Her thumb made small round circles on her desk.

Leaving as the moon releases, twig by twig the night entangled trees.

Night entangles trees. The sky would be a very intense dark blue black and the upper branches of the trees would stand out starkly against it, lit by the moon. She liked the idea of the sky being wrapped around the trees as if you could peel the night off and toss around the small pieces like candy floss. Would it float away or fall to the ground, she wondered?

Mr Banner's voice interrupted her thoughts.

For *love, the leaning grasses and two lights above the sea.*

She thought about the leaning grasses bending towards each other and the two lights like two people and how they loved each other and that lit up the world for them. Two little shining lights and how they glittered on the sea, their edges all blurry and they would look like one light really, wavering lines around it. She sighed. Two lights, one light, leaning grasses.

A poem should not mean, but be. he finished.

Silence stretched its long fingers up and down the aisles. Mr Banner looked into a sea of vacant faces. No-one spoke. Factory fodder, he thought. They'll be ruled by early buses and time-clocks. Furtive sex, shotgun weddings and the rest of their lives full of half-formed regrets they won't be able to grasp.

'What does this poem mean?' he asked. 'Come on, what does it mean? Did anyone enjoy it?'

'Yes, sir,' they chirruped.

'Well, what did you enjoy about it?'

'It was just good, sir,' Alice Sharrock ventured.

'Just good, girl, what do you mean, just good?'

'I don't know sir, I just liked the words, the sound of them...' She looked around desperately, wanting someone else to take over and get her out of this deep, dark hole she was fast digging for herself.

Mr Banner looked at Maureen. 'Are you dreaming there, girl?'

'No, sir.'

'Well, what do you think this poem meant?'

'It wasn't supposed to mean sir, it was supposed to be.'

Mr Banner's face went red. A vein pulsed near his ear.

'You're a lost cause, girl. What are you?'

'A lost cause, sir.'

'Just as long as we've got that straight.'

Maureen sat very still and looked attentive until he turned his back. Then she looked down. *Silent as the sleeve-worn stone of casement ledges where the moss had grown,* she read. Casement, a little window, wooden maybe, and it's mossy outside because no-one opens it any more. A little silent, secret window where you could watch the leaning grasses and two lights above the sea, where poems need not mean but be.

VIVIEN

Edmund Cusick

"This one's for you, Vivien," said Nigel, emerging from his office. Then, standing closer than I'd have liked, "Christ, you look hot. Everyone else wears T-shirts, you know. I assure you, my dear, I wouldn't mind seeing more of you."

I ignored the leer and opened it, a standard folder embossed, as usual, with our logo: the words *Millennium Heritage Trust* in gold, and a tower illuminated by a rising sun. Inside was a photocopy from the property pages of August's *Country Life*.

<u>Island Dream</u>
Private Island, thirty acres, 150 miles South West of Penzance. Period house (2 bedrooms), various outbuildings, own harbour. This unique property is of historic significance and unparalleled character.
Underneath, in his executive red ink, he'd written
    Status: Priority Purchase
    Surveyor: Vivien Hughes.

"You're joking," I said, as the door closed. My first survey. I should be excited, flattered, I knew. But that was what worried me. Why me? I'd only just been hired to do a bit of valuation. My background was fine art: I knew nothing about land. And I also knew damn well we wouldn't put a Priority Purchase on the Tower of London before the survey had been done. I steeled myself, called Niger's extension. He was smooth as ever.

"Of course I'm serious, Vivien. It's one of our obligations under the charter - preserve and protect, you know. Take your time over it, my dear."

It takes either a very good liar, or someone who's been lied to very well, to spot another. I qualified on both counts. If it had been legit, Nigel wouldn't have bothered being condescending, he'd just have told me to do my bloody job and be grateful. A scam of some sorts. I turned my face to the fan. God, it was hot.

Of course. August. In three weeks time the accounts would be closed for the year, as the season ended. The annual audit. I'd already wondered how we were going to cope with an embarrassing surplus in one of our current accounts. If HM treasurer should ever work out, as I had in a couple of months, that The Millennium Heritage Trust was not so much preserving and protecting the Nation's Property as dealing in it for profit then Nigel would find himself out of a job. Or worse.

We needed to buy something now, quickly, to get rid of the money. Purchasing ahead of survey was unheard of, but the sale would go through, our capital balance go down, and then, a month later, my survey would point out how mad the whole idea was, and he'd sell it. Take your time, he'd said. And then the money would find its way to one of Nigel's other little accounts. That was why he'd given it to me: hopelessly unqualified, unlikely to ask questions. And, if it came to it, easily overruled. I phoned him back, assumed the girly sycophancy he liked.

"Do some background work? Certainly, Vivien, we want a really thorough job. I'll authorise an account for you. Good-bye, my dear."

That simple. A week's paid leave. Expenses. Cornwall.

I wasn't extravagant. A decent business hotel, no wine on the bill, and I started work. A small donation from the trust account to the local antiquarian society, together with some professional flirting and some legally worthless hints of a larger donation to the county library, yielded a pile of documents I had no right to, and I retired to my room. After two days I had boiled it all down to three paragraphs.

Inys Morgen

Island formed of two granite outcrops, rising to 55m., situated 35.15 West, 40.28 North. Accessible by boat, from Penzance (8 hours) or St. Lyon (6 hours).

History: tradition holds Inys Morgen as the site of Celtic hermitage, variously dedicated to a number of female saints. Considered uninhabitable till, in 1884, an archaeological excavation, undertaken by The British and Cornish Archaeological Association, led by Thomas Trehearne, found evidence of fifth and sixth century habitation.

In 1887 Trehearne purchased the island and constructed the current house and harbour. After Trehearne's death in 1903 the island was bequeathed to the British and Cornish Archaeological Association. Requisitioned in 1940 for use as a long range navigation station for Coastal Command. Retained by the Ministry of Defence until Defence Review of 1999, when recommended for sale.

It was okay for Nigel but it left out the interesting bits. It didn't mention the peculiarities of the Reverend Enoch Trehearne, priest of the Church of England, father of eleven children, Freemason and founder member of the Hermetic Order of the Golden Dawn. From his long, gaunt face, the hollow eyes sunk in their sockets stared out at me from a hundred-year old photograph. Also gracing my desk was his masterwork, *Cornish Saints and the Arthurian Tradition,* a mixture of church history, legend, and lunacy. Then there was the British and Cornish Archaeological Association, responsible for financing the dig and then, bizarrely, the construction of new buildings on top of their prime site. Its benefactors, with modest unanimity, were anonymous. Its proceedings were unavailable, its accounts in private hands. Old Enoch could have taught Nigel a thing or two about organised fraud. I had to admire him.

The Sea Queen, out of Penzance, stank of cod and diesel. We sailed with the tide into the scarlet remains of sunset. The skipper took my money but refused all attempts at communication. It was a rough crossing. Rain came, and seasickness. I clung to a rail in the darkness. I had developed asthma in my teens and now it was a torment, breathing hard through heavy spray and sea-mist. Sleep was impossible and now I faced the devil's hours alone. 3 a.m. The hour the lies run thin, the hour not to be awake. The hour my parents had been killed, my father driving too late, too tired, they'd told me, and, I found out later, after one or two for the road. The hour I'd made my first attempt so that now I had to keep my wrists hidden, whatever Nigel liked. The hour I'd given up any hope of becoming an artist, acknowledging, at last, my lack of talent. Art had been my only religion, and that night I knew I had failed in it. Alone and shivering, I saw my life fall apart before my eyes, the past and then the future. I saw where it would end, the scams, the frauds, the plans getting more and more tangled and, through it all, my self-hatred growing, the sense of chances running out.

It was then that the water invited me. It would be swift. No more pain, just rest. I seized the rail, brought my weight up. But, with a gut-wrenching lurch, the boat pitched high, throwing me back onto the deck. I landed heavily on one knee, twisting it, and cried aloud. The sea, too, rejected me, and my courage failed.

With infinite slowness, the darkness thinned, and the fog grew from grey to white. The engine note changed. Then, out of the mist, a wall of rock, and, a minute later, a tiny harbour. For a man who had claimed no knowledge of the place, the skipper seemed to have a fine eye for navigating blind. A jetty of decaying concrete, draped in seaweed, reached out to us. Nauseous and shivering, I jumped, slipped, fell on the same knee I had hurt before, cursed with pain. The skipper watched, unmoved.

"Eight hours," he shouted.

I clung to the wet weed. A swish of wake, and he was gone. Cold. The slap of sea on rock. A path led up into the mist. I climbed unsteadily, limping. Each step brought pain. After a few precarious minutes, the path divided. Which way? I took the left hand fork, a thread of darkness in the white blur of mist. I climbed again, and saw the dark silhouette of a building. The house? I hobbled around it. A door. It pushed open, closed behind me under its own weight. Even breathing, in this damp, was hard. In pitch darkness I stepped forward and collided with something. My knee cracked against hard wood in front of me. It was then, spurred by the pain, that I slipped to the stone floor and started to cry.

When it was over, I felt the warm blood on my hands, the

shattered dial of my watch, cuts among the bruises. I had been beating my fists on the wood in front of me. Perhaps, if I was lucky, I would die here in the dark. My breathing was easier, as though some subtle change had passed in the air. I opened my eyes. Out of the gloom, a raw wound of colour was bleeding light: dancing in reds and greens. I stood up, and I knew where I was. I was in a chapel. Ahead of me was my salvation. A stained glass window.

The background was of brilliant emerald. Interlacing branches of green and black reached to the edge of the frame and on them were tiny flowers of pink and white. Three female figures stood tall enough to fill the frame. Their hair, gold, black and auburn by turns, fell to their waists, and each bore a circlet of silver. They wore garments that fell from breast to ankle, each of one colour, scarlet, blue, violet. Each, in medieval style, bore a token: she to the right, fair-haired, bore a wedge of golden honeycomb, and she to the left, whose hair was auburn, a single scarlet apple. The lady in the centre had a crown on her black hair. She bore a silver chalice. A trinity. I walked towards it, hesitated. I felt a strange sensation, a rushing wave as of cold air around me that settled in a knot of liquid cold in each palm as though I held melting ice in my hands. Slowly I approached the altar. I made out a decanter of dark wine. I lifted the cold weight of the stopper, dipped my finger, tasted, smiled with surprise. I looked up. The Queen looked back at me with slanted, violet eyes. The mouth was cold. Whatever - whoever - was represented there was not human. A fairy queen or demoness? There was apple blossom behind her but this was not Eden. I looked again behind the offered apple in the left hand panel. There was no coiled snake. No sin. Only honey. This was a pagan fruit - the apple of the Otherworld. What did they call it?

Avalon. The Isle of Avalon. Paradise. The sea boomed again. A single drop of golden honey seemed to drip from one finger, glowing like amber.

It was a Burne-Jones. There was no mistaking it. The Quest of the Sangraal series. And this one was unknown, the fulfilment of them all. God. It would be a nine-day sensation. A lost masterpiece discovered on the furthest flung piece of England. The M.o.D. would look pretty silly. Hadn't the RAF ever looked in here? Of course. Various outbuildings. To them, it would just be another piece of church glass. The last Burne-Jones in a lost chapel in the sea. The Art press would go berserk and, after them, the Quality Sundays. The whole island would become a national treasure. Nigel would make a killing.

If I told him.

It wouldn't be hard. I still knew people from College - the successful ones - people who knew people. A trip to London. A deal. After my report, the trust would sell the whole island and a gallery could buy it through some innocuous third party. And, in return, I could name my price. Not money. A job - something I believed in. Valuation, perhaps, or my own gallery. I was looking at my salvation. All this passed through my mind in seconds.

I tore myself away. Outside, my eyes were dazzled by the sun. The mist had gone and I saw the island laid out beneath me, bare as another St Kilda. I stood on the shoulder of one of the two rocky crests. Beneath, in the waist of low land between them, lay the house and, below it, the harbour. Still half-blind in the glare, I saw a tangled spiral of barbed wire gleaming like a spider's web in steel. The incongruity of war in such a place. I felt, somehow, immeasurable relief, lightness, to be here, now. My knee seemed better. A little unsteadily, I walked down to the house. It had stood up well to the Atlantic gales though there were tiles missing, paint peeling. A wooden door. I pushed through it, to a kitchen. A squat black stove. A whisky bottle on the windowsill, the cap unbroken. A table with a tea-pot, two clean cups. There was a man sitting in an ancient arm chair. There was something about his long, thin features that seemed familiar, and for a moment another picture flashed into my mind. His eyes were closed. As I looked, unbelieving, they opened, regarding me as though half-focused.

"Would you like a cup of tea?"

I had almost screamed but he had stayed seated and that reassured me. He was offering me a cup of tea. Then I saw his hands tremble. Christ, he was more frightened than I was. But the voice, the eyes, were kind, if troubled. My instinct told me he was not dangerous. Probably. I relaxed a fraction.

"Sorry to startle you," he said "I was...um asleep."

He was not a good liar which, in its way, reassured me, whatever he had been doing. The voice was gentle, the accent somewhere between Truro and Sloane Square. So were the clothes: tweed jacket, heavy boots, faded cord trousers, a check shirt.

"Why didn't you let me know there was someone here? You must have heard the bloody boat!"

"Yes. But I thought you'd come here straight away. That's why I made you some tea." - he gestured to the table - "but I hadn't reckoned on the mist. You went the other way, up to the chapel, and I didn't want to...to disturb you there."

But it was the chapel, not me, I sensed, which needed to be left undisturbed.

"Yes," I said. "It's quite a place."

"Indeed, Miss Hughes."

I tensed.

"Sorry. Penzance is a small place. You're Vivien Hughes, aren't you, from the Millennium Heritage Trust? We heard you were coming out here."

"Oh? We being..."

"The British and Cornish Archaeological Association. I expect you've heard of us if you've been looking into the island's history."

"Yes. The Reverend Trehearne. But only until 1940. Are you telling me you're still going?"

"That's right."

"And now the M.o.D. is selling the place, you're trying to come back?"

"Not exactly. The thing is, we never really left."

"Never?"

"Well, during the war, of course. But even then the place was never garrisoned. They never built their radar, in the end."

Something about his assurance irritated me.

"Is the Ministry of Defence aware that you're in illegal occupation of restricted crown property?"

"No. But I doubt they'd mind, now."

"We might, though. You know we have certain special privileges, Mr..."

"Simon'll do."

"Well, Simon, under our charter we can put a compulsory purchase order on this place if we feel its heritage value is under threat. Neat, isn't it? So the...um...Association might find itself without a home."

I knew I'd scored then, but he seemed to keep his cool.

"Quite. Quite so. That's why you're here. And will you buy it?"

"Yes. I'm here to survey it."

His hands shook slightly, I saw, and he pushed them into his pockets.

"Oh."

Neither of us spoke. Through the door behind me I could hear the swell breaking on the rocks. Of course, *The Sea Queen* would have brought him here. Perhaps other boats, too. They would be well paid for keeping quiet. And for bringing supplies in, too, presumably.

We both let the silence linger. Then curiosity overcame me. The Burne-Jones. *The Sleep of Arthur in Avalon* ... the one the world thought he had died painting, giving the last of his strength to it.

"That window? It's uncatalogued. Was it the last thing he designed?"

"It was a private gift."

"A private...? God, you're not saying he was in your association - Avalon, the works?"

"He was very interested in the Arthurian tradition," he said, choosing his words. Then, as though quoting, "I am at Avalon, not yet in Avalon..."

Once again his condescension infuriated me.

"I know the line. Letter to Georgiana, the summer before he died."

"You're an expert?"

"It's what I'm paid for."

I paused, letting things click together.

"So you really believe this place is Avalon ? That's what Trehearne was on about, underneath it all? This lump of rock? You're mad."

He was quiet for so long that I began to listen again to the sea, rising and breaking, falling and rising against the shore. When he spoke, I barely heard him at first.

"The dig we did in 1884 - you know about it?"

I nodded.

"There were a lot of pieces of fine glass. Apothecaries' phials. A pestle, parts of a mortar. It was a place of healing. And it was a shrine, we know that, don't ask me how. All this is Fifth, Sixth Century. If a king - Arthur, say - was wounded and the mainland was over-run, this would have been the obvious place to bring him."

"But Avalon? It's only a myth."

"Better for people to think that, if the king was here."

"But Paradise - the Isle of Apples?"

"The sea level's risen since the sixth century. Most of the old island is under the sea. As for apples, the Romans had vines in Cornwall, - apricots, even. It was warmer then. We know they had an orchard here."

His sureness irritated me, as did the well-rehearsed lunacy.

"So your Association came across one of the most important Dark Age sites in Britain and published a pack of lies? Some nonsense about a minor Celtic hermitage?"

"The secret - the dig, that is - had come to us in a special way. We wanted to keep it special. The Association has - had - other interests."

"I know." My mind leaped to Enoch's biography. The Order of the Golden Dawn. It was still going on.

"You're all into the occult, aren't you?"

For the first time I knew I had the advantage. His face went blank with surprise.

"Yes, if you want to put it like that. Magic is probably an easier word. Less Gothic Horror, as it were."

I looked at the old tweed, the sad, hollow hazel eyes, the tea pot. The nervous hands.

"Don't worry. I can't exactly see you sacrificing black cockerels under a full moon."

He kept a straight face. "Oh, I don't know...now and again."

We laughed, then, together, the only time, and his thin, elongated face looked years younger. I found it hard to stop laughing: the delayed shock of the meeting, all that had happened in the chapel, the tension between us, all releasing. Not that I trusted him. But we drank tea, in Avalon. He was younger than he looked, only thirty. Had been a land agent in Devon. Before that, once, an engraver, but had given it up. Now he was guardian of the island, whatever that meant. He knew something about art. Less than me.

"So do you have rituals here?"

He seemed to choose his words. "We have meditations."

"What for?"

"You'd laugh, Miss Hughes."

"Probably. Tell me anyway."

"For Britain, for its spiritual welfare."

"If you've been doing them since the 1880s, they don't seem to have done much good."

"Oh I don't know. They brought you out here."

Was this flirting ? It seemed out of character.

"That's very flattering but I was sent by my boss. On the off-chance that we might turn the place into a theme park - the Hermitage experience, perhaps."

I looked out of the window to where a line of turquoise waves was curving like a lens of glass, holding the rock for a second in its reflection.

"God, if Nigel knew what you'd told me. The genuine Avalon. He'd rebuild it from scratch. Teenagers on youth training schemes in plastic armour. Fibreglass battlements. Wenches. All cleavage and mulled wine. It'd make Tintagel look like the British Museum."

I stopped, suddenly angry. "Why did you tell me? I can tell them all this, you know. Or get the place excavated again. Christ, you know we're about to buy it! Why trust me?"

"Because of what happened in the chapel"

"How do you know what happened there?"

Now he was quiet again, almost grave.

"How long were you in there?"

I looked down. The watch was broken, of course, all jagged glass. I looked outside at the sun. It seemed higher, somehow, than it should have been

"Half an hour? Three quarters? What's that got to - "

"Four and a half hours?"

"No."

I stood up and went to the window. Had I passed out? I must have. Had he heard me screaming? It would seem not. God, what a mess.

"So will you tell them," he asked.

"Avalon? No, I won't tell them. We've destroyed enough places as it is."

"Thank you, Miss Hughes."

Why did he have to thank me? My own plan, the trip to London, the gallery. That deal would tear this place apart, just as effectively, though less obviously. They'd rip out the window and ship it back to London. Or they'd turn this place into an offshore St. Ives. Cultural Tourism. Guide books instead of candy floss.

Either way, his island, their island, would disappear. A century of peace here, of the chapel, their crazy rituals. And I would destroy it. I knew. I had to.

"Let me show you the island?"

"Okay."

Outside the sun was hot. We climbed to the other tiny summit, looked over to the chapel. All around the sea held us, enchanted. The sun, the wind were intoxicating and I rolled up my sleeves, stopped. His eyes flicked down, then looked away. I hated him then, hating him and the red scars on my white flesh equally. I would destroy them both, destroy him, and the past. I knew that. I would do it. He was still looking away while I fumbled with my cuffs.

"Did you read the inscription in the chapel?" he asked, not looking at me.

"I didn't see one."

"'For him who finds me, I shall heal all wounds.'"

I was fighting more tears now, furious at his pity.

"Healed you then, has it ? Or are you still drying out?"

His shoulders flinched.

Neither of us spoke.

Then he asked, "Is it that obvious?"

"I notice things. There's grape juice in the chapel instead of communion wine. The whisky in the kitchen - that's a kind of test, isn't it ? And who gives up engraving to be a land agent, for God's sake ? You lost it all."

"Yes."

"And don't expect me to be sorry. I've had enough from liars. And drunks. My father, amongst others."

We were silent again, for a long time. Each listening to the sea;

and not listening.

"So all this business about the Association. Aren't they a bit crazy to let you look after this place? If it's so important?"

He was angry now, which was what I wanted, I think. To smash through the charm, the pretence. But he kept his voice almost calm.

"'For him who finds me' - there's a tradition that the keeper of the island is someone who has some injury, some wound. Our founder- Trehearne. He had TB. But this place kept him alive, cured him. This is my wound, in a way. And - I'm trusted.

"And being a descendant of the great man helps, I suppose?"

"God. Where do you come from?" Again his voice was shocked. I was almost satisfied.

"The big world. I've had his photo on my desk for the last week. There's a resemblance. I've also read his correspondence."

"How did you get hold of that?" The anger was barely controlled now.

"The usual. Flirting. Money."

Far away, a faint stuttering sounded on the air. I looked at my watch, useless. Eight hours? It could not be. But perhaps, here, it could. *The Sea Queen* was in sight, a white flicker of bow-wave, the square cabin.

"I'm going.'

"Yes," he said.

We looked at each other, the two of us half-sick with anger, hatred. I walked away, and he followed. The sound of the engine echoed off the concrete jetty. The skipper raised his hand in a gesture that was more salute than greeting. Suddenly the whole thing seemed wrong. All of it. And it already seemed half-real. The chapel, this man alone in his hermitage, the violence of my attack, the need to destroy him. I did not understand.

The wake splashed against the quay and an unfriendly hand reached out to grab me aboard. This was wrong, all wrong. I turned back and, without warning, he kissed me. Not with affection, still less with desire. I cannot describe that kiss - his lips pressed on mine for barely a second; chaste, detached. Neither forgiveness nor anger in them. I did not understand.

The journey back was smooth enough. I had time to think. it was him or me. I needed that island, as he did. Through it, through that window, I would save myself. The last Burne-Jones. I would give Nigel the report he wanted. And I would go to London. The place would be sold within a year of my report, and then someone would buy it, anonymously. And then I'd move. We - myself and my chosen gallery - would buy the place for a song, and go public the day after. I'd have the life I'd dreamed of.

And the Association and Simon would be finished. Why did I want that, too, now ? But I did.

That night in the hotel I slept more soundly than I had done for a year and, for once, my dreams were sweet. I was in the chapel. And the Queen with the mocking eyes stepped forward with the grail and pressed it to my lips, and I drank. I understood. I could have all that I wanted. I wrote two letters. One, typed, to be faxed to Nigel. Mission accomplished. The other, by hand, I posted care of *The Sea Queen*, Penzance. Then I fell ill.

Nigel rang the morning I was back.

"I've read the report, Vivien. Good work. Shame that it was delayed by your flu. Obviously we wouldn't have bought the place if we'd been able to read your recommendations earlier. As you say, setting up our own transport out there would take us beyond the writ of the charter, whatever its attractions. Still, I'm sure we can sell it, sometime."

I waited, though each day was a greater torment. Then, four months later, Nigel made his move and put the island on the market. We sold at a slight profit to a firm of solicitors, and Nigel acquired a Jaguar. That day I resigned from the trust.

This time the skipper greeted me, offering the same salute I had seen once before.

It was an easier crossing. The whisky was gone from the window but Simon had left it in the cupboard for me. A farewell present. Now I have the solitude I have craved for so long. One day I will leave, to what, I don't know. The Association will look after me. For now, I have time.

And I am starting to heal.

SAYING HELLO TO THE BIRDS

Heather Leach

They've put up a new bus stop. There's that Pakistani lady from the papershop, Mrs Siddiqui, waiting in it when I get there.

"Very nice, very nice," she says, trying it all out, sitting on the seat and touching the glass sides, " but the boys will break it, I think."

There's this poem on the bus shelter and a picture of Shakespeare with long hair and a beard.

We used to do poems at school. The teacher, Mrs Aspinall, only the lads called her Mrs Asitall, because she'd got big boobs, used to read out poems. When she comes into the classroom, Nikko Tomlinson says, "Don't bother trying anything fancy Miss, because we've had everything. We've had films, tape recordings, making plays, sex talks, going on trips and we don't want to be arsed doing anything else."

She says, "I won't do anything fancy then, I'll just read you some poetry."

So we all go, "Oh God, bloody hell", and some of the lads put their heads on the tables, and Janice McCran switches her Walkman up so everybody can hear the bass, and it sounds like a big machine thumping under the classroom floor. Mrs Aspinall was scared of us at first, you could see her hands shaking. She reads a poem, then she asks us what we think about it, and nobody says anything, well, nothing about the poem. There's plenty being said about how Nikko's had it off last night with Teresa Reece from the third year. I went out with him once. He didn't try anything, Just got me a packet of chips and walked round the precinct for two hours talking about football. Mrs Aspinall never raised her voice, even with all that racket, just carried on reading and reading.

Waiting at the bus stop, I get into studying the poem. I can't make most of it out. It starts *Shall I compare thee to a summer's day* ... and I keep staring and staring at it until I hear Mrs Siddiqui saying, "You will be missing the bus, hurry, hurry," and she's on the step, and the bus driver's going on as well, "Take it or bloody leave it, girl, I haven't got all day."

I sit on the seat which is supposed to be for the disabled. There's nowhere else and you feel a bit funny, with that notice, *Please leave this space for people with limited mobility,* next to your left ear. Everywhere you look there's writing. On this bus: *Design your Own Course at the Adult Education College; Cinderella Comes to the Palace at Christmas; Use the Bus and Save the Environment.* You can't rest your eyes anywhere without reading something.

I learned to read dead quick when I was a little kid, but sometimes I wish I hadn't bothered, because it seems like all reading is good for is to give strangers free passage into your brain.

On that journey, it's all the same for miles, blocks of flats with grass in between, broken buildings and little rows of shops. Churches turned into warehouses and the warehouses up for sale. The shops aren't much cop, newsagents with cages over dirty windows, second hand washing machines on the pavements, bookies and video places, that's about it. But surprise, surprise, there's one of the new shelters at every bus stop with proper little roofs, glass sides and nice benches to sit on. All the way up the road, there's people on them seats looking pleased with themselves, and when they get on the bus it's all anybody talks about.

"Who's put them up?" this woman in a green scarf says to the driver.

"Nothing to do with me," he says. "I just drive, they don't tell me nothing."

A right charmer he is. You either seem to get that type, misery on toast, or the other kind, the one who keeps hold of your hand when you give him the money, and tries to get everybody singing. Either way it's a dead pain.

Green scarf woman sits behind me and starts talking to the bloke next to her, "It's about time they did something about them shelters. We've been stood in broken glass for months, and that graffiti, it's disgusting, you should see what was wrote on the old shelter. Mind you they won't last. Nothing lasts round here."

That starts them all off about the youth, no discipline and it's the parents I blame, as if half of them didn't have kids themselves, wagging off school and nicking boilers out of empty houses. I look across at Mrs Siddiqui but she's not silly enough to say anything about the boys here.

Green scarf's still talking, "Did you see what they've put on it?" she says. "It's a bloody poem. Who thought of that daft idea? It's our money that goes on poems, you know."

I have a look at the next stop, and she's right. All the new shelters have got old Shakespeare on them, his funny little bald head floating and the words in lines underneath, black lines on white paper, no colours or anything. I thought it might be different poems, but then I get the first couple of lines,

Shall I compare thee to a summers day,

Thou art more lovely . . .

It's that one. They've put the same poem on them new bus shelters all the way up the Oldham Road.

It's raining outside. The bus smells of rubbery clothes, and the windows steam up. The windscreen wipers swish swish and it feels dead cosy in there. The voices are still droning away behind me, but I can't hear what they're saying anymore. I lean my face on the cold glass and make a hole in the steam with my fingers. From where I'm sitting I can get a good view of it, that poem, and I start trying to get the words in my head. Even though half of its crap, I can't stop learning it. It gets to be a thing with me, like touching all the lamp posts on the way home. I used to do that when I was a little kid. I used to think, if I touch all the lampposts and say all the numbers right, when I get in there won't be any arguments going on, my dad won't be pissed, and my Mam'll have chips for my tea. I still do it sometimes coming back from the dole or Bazzer's, stupid really.

By the time we get to the old Brewery, I'm up to this bit about the darling buds of May. You don't see many buds round here. Most of the plants are the kind the council puts in, hard leaves with sharp edges and all the rubbish gets stuck round them. Then the next line has something about Summer's lease being too short and you can say that again. The only way anybody knows it's summer round our way, is when the Spinner's Arms puts a table and two chairs out on the pavement, when the ice-cream van's still ringing its bell after

News at Ten and the Bacardi advert goes up on the railway bridge.

Sitting on that seat, I keep hearing Bazzer's voice in my head "What's the problem with us getting together? " he says. "You can't keep saying you don't know, Carol, you've got to have a reason." It's all he ever talks about these days, when he's not on about smashing the state or who's won the snooker. I do like him, he's got a bit more about him than a lot of the other lads. He says it'll change soon, people'll start burning the place down.

I said , "What do you want to get a flat for if it's going to get burned down?" Only he thinks I'm trying to be clever so he doesn't answer. My Mam's on his side.

"She always was Miss Shilly-Shally, Bazzer, our Miss Fancy-Pants Carol. It's that what's started her on this buses lark."

I manage to get another line in before we get to Piccadilly,
Sometime too hot the eye of heaven shines
I hate it when it's hot. You get everybody standing out on the pavement, sitting on their front steps, leaning over the balconies, and all the dust and the dog shit gets up your nose. The lads start driving round the estate like maniacs, burning the tyres and the police chase after them, so it's like a race track. You'd think it'd be better in the summer, but it isn't. The blue sky makes it look worse and you can't go anywhere, but you can't stop in either. You sit on the maisonette steps and you see planes going over, little silver tubes floating high up. They don't make a sound until they've gone past, as if they were trying to get away with it. Watching them planes makes you feel as if you're living at the bottom of a dirty big pit. The men come and spray the pavement to kill off the weeds, and they mow the bits of grass round the edges and afterwards

there's hundreds of daisies lying with their heads cut off. I like it when it's raining, when you can't see far, when the cloud comes down low so that it all looks the same, and you don't have to worry about anything different.

In Piccadilly there's that same poem at each stop. It looks a bit stupid really, them white posters everywhere, but most people aren't taking any notice. It's stopped raining so I go and sit in the gardens for a bit. There's an old feller asleep on one of the seats, and a woman with piles of carrier bags, but they don't bother me.

I can hear Bazzer talking in my head again, "There's loads of nutters about, you know. I don't like you going to them places on your own."

I'd like to talk to the woman with the bags. I'd like to ask her where she comes from, where she's going next, but everytime anybody goes near her she waves her arms and shouts, so I leave her alone. I sit there and say the poem, the bits of it I can remember, over in my head. It's like being on an island, buses and cars going round and round, and then this big drill starts where they're digging up the road, and birds fly up off the trees, hundreds of them in a black swarm, and then they come down again rattling and chattering nearly as loud as the drill. Nobody seems to be taking any notice of the birds either but then I catch sight of the carrier bag woman and she's looking at them with a little bit of a smile on her face as if she knew them, as it they were old friends who'd just dropped in for a nice cup of tea.

It starts pissing down hard again so I set off back to the bus. My Mam says, "This is what I can't understand about it, Carol, you don't do anything when you get there, you just turn round and come back. I wouldn't mind if you were doing something useful I think you're going a bit soft, girl. They'll be having you in the Psychiatric next."

Me and Shirley used to think it was dead good in Town. We went in all the shops and in the Arndale. That's where she met that Wythenshawe lad, sitting near the fountains. I used to think there was something there I wanted and couldn't have. Bazzer says, "All that bloody stuff, all them videos and music centres, it's ours as much as theirs."

He and my Mam go up regular and come back with a load of gear, pockets full of it, whatever they can nick. Me and Shirley used to do it as well, but I can't be bothered now. I think Mam might be right. I'm going to end up like that carrier bag woman if I'm not careful, sitting on benches and saying hello to the birds.

On the way back there's more people standing in the bus shelters, some of them not even waiting for buses, just keeping out of the rain. I want to shout at them, "Get out of the bloody way, I can't see the poem. By the time we get to the old chimney, I'm nearly at the end,

Nor shall death brag...

I used to think about dying a lot. You look at old people and it suddenly dawns on you that they haven't always been like that. I started my periods and that was it,

"You can't go running about the streets now, you know, " Mam said, and I had to stay in or lean on walls like the older girls or sit on the maisonette steps talking. Nobody ever used to say anything about death, but I thought about it all the time. I'd wake up in the night and lie there wondering what it was I'd forgotten. Then I'd remember and I could never go back to sleep again after that.

When I get off at our stop, I sit on the seat reading the poem over and over. I can't make out what the last part means,
...so long lives this and this gives life to thee
I used to get really pissed off with some of them poems that Mrs Aspinall read,

"Why don't they write them in bloody English, Miss?' She says, "You'll have to write your own, Carol," and Nikko Booth starts singing, "Carol is a barrel," so I give him, "Nikko is a dicko," and then the bell goes so that's the end of that. It starts going dark in the shelter and the poem gets dim but it's in my head now so it doesn't matter. Somebody's written Man United in black felt tip on the glass so while I'm sitting there I scratch CAROL in little letters on the back of the seat with my nail file. Lots of buses come and go, but I still stop there, until that Mrs Siddiqui gets off,

"What is the matter? Here you are again," she says and she can see I've been crying my bloody eyes out, and I feel a right fool skriking like a kid in a bus shelter.

I told Bazzer I wasn't going down the housing. He was dead pissed off. He wants to get away from his dad and who can blame him, but I says, "I'm not going so you can forget it."

My Mam says I'll have to find somewhere else anyway, "You're too big to stop at home at your age."

I think she's thinking about shacking up with the bloke who catches Ping-Pong balls at the bingo. He's got two kids of his own so I can see the way her mind's bending.

Next week when I get my dole money I'm going on a bus that goes the other way. I'll see if there's anything different up there. It looks the same, but you never know. They've got adverts in the bus shelters now. At our stop there's one for Lean Cuisine Dinners where the poem used to be.

"They won't be putting any more poems in," says one of the drivers. "They only had one set, that Shakespeare feller, and they only put him in until they'd got enough adverts." He says this while the bus's going along and all the people sitting on the bottom deck who can hear him, have a good laugh at the idea of anybody giving a bugger.

AN UN-INHABITED ISLAND

Neil O'Donnell

Act I, scene 1: Alive.
The planes drift into the blue every ten minutes as if being teased to the ground by some fine, tense cord. They are pulled into the insignificance of the steel metropolis, discharged from air to land then ocean in one sweeping movement.

Adrift, a speckle on the horizon, the city falls into a flat horizon. The distance between them grows.

One reads beside the other without expression or movement, holding the pen that accompanies him through all his routines. Later, when it is dark, with the same pen, he will form his own letters into words on a page. Meanwhile, the other is silent. Searching for a clearer thought, he gapes over the waves. He is sure the pillars of steel are shimmering as they recede.

The other is uncertain whether it is the heat which ripples the horizon or the swaying of the boat which causes this. He is unsure. It does not trouble him.

They met in Bangkok. One was coughing and remained silent about the pink red sores that littered his genitals and anus. They would fade by the time they reached Penang.

The other was nervous and itchy about his new adventure. He sweats too much, a state not helped by his hair-covered body.

Medically interesting. Me and Him.

What they began in Bangkok - their friendship - has brought them this far. Along the curve of Thailand, then from the airport in Malaysia, to this floating stage set: a low ferry, from Singapore to Jakarta. One in silent thought, the other silently reading thoughts. Perhaps they should join forces and confer? Hold a public debate on the starboard deck? Invite the four-hundred or so Asian faces to judge their rhetoric?

The other asks, "So how do you see life near the millennium?"

One: *The solemn temples, the great globe itself,*
Yeah, all which it inherit, shall dissolve,
And, like the insubstantial pageant faded,
Leave not a rack behind. We are such stuff
As dreams are made on; our little life
Is rounded with a sleep.

Act I, scene 2: The First Morning Adrift.

The massive ferry scissors through the Berhala Straight, along the coast of Sumatra, keeping a safe distance from the coastline, they are close enough to see the flat, dark oval of the shore. As before, they sit on the raised deck, observing the wake. Two perfectly straight, isolated furrows in the ocean gently drowning away from each other.

Sitting on the left.

"Which came first. The orange or the Orang-utan?"

Although they are alone, the other one has not heard. The volume of his novel needs reducing.

He tries again. "Where are all the people from below? Why do they never appear?"

"Perhaps they have seen all this before."

"But there is nothing to see."

"Exactly."

Act II, scene 1: Below.

Their bunks oppose each other. They kill time at night - the only time they spend beneath the deck - with games of backgammon and draughts. The other cannot play chess. Amongst the cleared-out deck and the light brown patient faces, they rattle dice and think of sweeping moves and diagonal conquests.

A man, also in his early twenties, occasionally stands to the left of them and lifts his artificial bladder. The thick clear tube hangs in a sad u-bend. One strains his eyes to witness the event, the other concentrates on the game.

The two men are together, travelling beside each other for reasons of ease and convenience. Their divided histories, before the departure, have only been released in hints and half sentences that always threatened to reveal too much about themselves. They have reached that part of a relationship where ignorance is expected, where answers are no longer required. The need has expired.

"Are there any sharks in the South China Sea?"

"Why would there not be?"

One has a girlfriend on the northern side of the equator. He tells the other that she understood his need to see the world. To educate himself. He is playing the part of the wandering soul, acting at travelling before donning a suit for the job which his education has rehearsed him for.

The other has never held a woman. "But if I did", he thought,

"I would not release her for a broader horizon." The other has flirted with education. He would like to be able to correspond or spend time in the second-hand book stalls, gazing at the vertical titles before slowly removing one for inspection.

"And yet," he thinks, "I am in the same position as him. I am travelling and why is it so bad that I have nothing to go back for? What use is a temporary escape?"

Chalk and cheese. Me and Him. Heads and tails. Slugs and snails.

Act II, scene 2: Deeper.

On a boat, where can a man walk except on water?

So the other explores below the decks, deep beneath the surface of the massive steel air bubble. The hum of the atmosphere seems to guide him but he has no idea of this or where he is going. It is a strangely silent hum. Like the sound of thoughts within a skull that could almost drive a man insane.

He imagines a vicious storm. Above, where the masses sleep, the turmoil would wash everyone and everything together. The objects would crash and collide. Yet here, he would be able to glide and judge his flight as he bounces off the smooth hull. Alive and aware of the danger.

"I would still drown," he mutters to himself. "Although, down here, my body might not be found."

"I see you've found the first class deck. Hi, my name is Ariel."

She stands before him and against a riveted background. Her words echo through the hull, surround his body. She has uncontrollable red hair and small freckles litter her skin. Like an animal she flicks her eyes around the subject of her focus. He stares without intention and immediately falls in love with the idea of loving her.

They talk.

Ariel unknowingly seduces him with her history. Tales of drunken flights and imprisonment flow from her like a sweet perfume.

He is enchanted.

Ariel tells him that she has never been free and he immediately wants to possess her.

"But you're alone." he tells her, "travelling as you please. You are as free as anyone on this earth. You can decide your own fate."

She replies that they are within the hull of this giant vessel that has only one destination.

"I cannot even swim," she tells him. "And where can one walk upon a boat, except on water?"

She kisses him and disappears.

Act II, scene 3: Above But Still Below.

The other one is ill. The fever sweeps his body. His eyes are sore, his joints are stiff. His book lies beside him and his crook-like pen has fallen from his limp hand. The endless rows of Indonesians are mostly ignorant of his condition.

The other appears from the abandoned deck and the man carrying his bladder stares at him with a concerned look.

"Are you all right?" The other whispers the words delicately.

"Not exactly. I feel a bit drowned - I mean, down."

"I'll get the doctor. There must be a doctor."

And there is. A small uniformed man with a slight moustache whose broken English is too fast for them to fully understand. He looks at the flaccid body beneath the single white sheet and diagnoses a case of Western Stomach: food poisoning.

Later the British Consulate in Jakarta will ask this Doctor if he remembers the case.

"Of course.," he will say. "Did they not both die on board?"

Act III, scene 1: Returning to the Deck Below.

The other has left his companion in a light slumber and has returned to where Ariel sleeps. He tells her that his friend is ill and she suggests that they should move him to this quieter level. The other dismisses her idea with a mumble. It lies deep within him, this conviction, that they should never meet.

"What does the Doctor say?" she asks him.

"That it is food poisoning. That it will pass. That he will be okay."

"How long have you known him ?"

"Just a few months."

Act III, scene 2: That Night, Below the Surface.

He beckons the other to his side.

"I am ill."

His words are like a plea. He looks lost, adrift.

"My mind is disappearing, as are my eyes and movement. I see strangers. I hear words that are not my own."

He seems ghostly.

"Look upon me."

He gestures at the other to remove the shroud that clings to his obscene damp body.

"Look upon me."

The other now stands above a rack of damp bones. He stares, full of pity.

"Reveal my disease."

The other gently lifts and folds down the stained underwear. Hesitantly, he uncovers the infection. Weeping red sores crawl across the scattering of sodden hair. He searches for some sign to tell him that it is not as bad as it appears.

"I'll get the doctor," is the only response he can make.

And the ruffled doctor enters, takes one glance, announces, "Quarantine. Lower deck. Move," as if the words are a well-rehearsed formula, only of use in that certain order.

Act IV, scene 1: Which is Where They Met.

Ariel hears the sounds of movement and the voices of men. She remains quiet and hesitant. The noise of the four men transferring a mattress with a semi-conscious passenger reminds her of home and the moment she threw her belongings, wrapped in a sheet, from a window and fled.

After twenty minutes of silence, she creeps towards the body.

"I thought you were dead."

Although he is conscious, he does not respond.

"I've met your friend," she states proudly. "He said you were ill but he said it was just food poisoning, that you would be okay. This, whatever this is, is more than food poisoning."

Ariel sits on the edge of his bunk, immediately feels at ease, her legs loosely crossed, and begins a conversation she gladly dominates. He only interrupts with brief comments. His eyes never leave her profile.

Ariel reveals her history of past abuse and imprisonment by

parents and various lovers. She unfolds her life before this silent audience of one. The times when she felt like reaching for the clouds or like gliding to an instant death. Her lines are spoken with a blank passion that masks her torment.

"I have always been loved to the point of suffocation," she tells him. "Held too tight. Secured by words. Kept."

He listens and decides that hers, whoever she is, will be the last face that he will see.

Act IV, scene 2: Through a Steel Door.

Jealous, excluded from such strange intimacy, the other stands and listens to Ariel and her reel of language.

When he was a child he often stood like this, outside a scene. His parents would argue and he would stand in a corridor, afraid to make a sound, afraid to be part of the reason.

"Why can she not tell me these things? I have known her longer and she has never told me. Is it because he is ill?. Is that it? Yes, that's it? She has fallen in love with him because he is helpless but she knew me first."

He departs on his tip-toes and returns to the deck to rifle through the large rucksack which holds too many books for a backpacker to haul. They do not interest him. Reading does not interest him. Yet he is drawn to the pages of the journal that, even in his sickness, his friend has so copiously filled.

Act IV, scene 3: Simultaneously.

The patient is revealing a history. He lights her heart with the prologue of an ignorant man whose innocence ruled his action. A story of a fool stumbling through the world without any concept of his being. A man of pure chance. A man shaped by a void in his past. A beast unaware of any form of pleasure. He blackens Ariel's listening heart with the idea of hate and destruction. Blame is placed on his terminal condition and a remedy is offered.

A devil, a born devil, on whose nature
Nurture can never stick; on whom my pains,
Humanely taken, all, all lost, quite lost;
And as with age his body uglier grows,
So his mind cankers. I will plague them all,

Act V, scene 1: In a Moment.

Ariel has her instructions. Without question she will obey. For two days he has been pouring his delirious soul upon her lap. He has entrapped her with his rambling of faith, fortune and destiny, controlling her with infectious, incapable promises.

Thou shalt be free
As mountain winds: but then exactly do
All points of my command.

Ariel can only believe him. Strange how entrapment causes such belief in freedom.

Act V, scene 2: The Scene is Set.

In the clear night Ariel lies beside the other on the deck. The stars are placed in a pattern that appears to swirl towards them with each movement of the boat.

The violent manner of her taking of him had surprised him. She had held him and discharged him in what had seemed an instant. There had been no words, just a gliding hand and a look of unmistakable submission. Within the surrounding half-candle darkness, she had sat across him on the raised steel seating. Her breath had interacted with the thrust of the waves from the ship. It had been as intense and tender as it had been tragic.

Epilogue: Now, in Present Time.

Ariel reaches into the tight pocket of her loose jacket for the instrument and uses her thumb to arm the weapon with a deft click. Then, in one swift movement, she arcs her upper body. Her hair rises and spreads like flames in the space between them. The fist hits the centre of his neck and the tightly-gripped pen is submerged in his windpipe. Ariel stands back, chooses not to witness the choking, bloody scramble behind her, and strolls away.

In a few minutes, as instructed, she will drag the body and the journal and feed them to the ocean. Then Ariel will wash the small area of deck and return to her instructor's deathbed.

She will find him and his promises dead. Ariel will then fade like a ripple in the ocean.

Me and him. Half-man, half-beast. Oil and water. One light, one deep.

Exeunt

ECHO SHOES

Aileen La Tourette

"We could go to Ferragamo first," Ruth suggests hopefully. "Just to have a look?"

Jackie hesitates. Would it hurt so much, to detour the old bag to an Italian shoe emporium for half an hour? Well, it would.

"Once we go there, you'll never buy the Ecco shoes," she thinks of the name as she says it. She assumes it isn't spelled like echo. "It will put you off even more."

"Nothing could put me off more. I am put off already to the ultimate degree," Ruth says honestly, smiling. She wants desperately to visit the shop with the wood floors polished and shining like gold satin ribbons, the shoes like little vessels for drinking out of, for dancing in, not mere humdrum walking. For collecting like shells on the golden, polished beaches of her childhood and displaying, proudly. Only the shoes would be displayed in a neat shoe-bag on the inside of her wardrobe door, each one with its wood and wire shoe-tree tucked inside. She loves good shoes. Really good shoes are precious, small things like babies, like her adored twin grandsons, identical but also different, like the right foot and the left.

"Oh fuck, all right."

"Pardon?"

"I'll call the cab." *You skinny little Rumanian bitch.* Jackie goes to the phone and dials the number from a card her ex-mother-in-law holds up in front of her. It's a special cab service for the elderly who have the good fortune to reside in the borough of Westminster. *There goes my day.* And when I leave you at six or seven or eight, *when I prise myself away, you'll make me feel guilty anyway, you old Transylvanian vampire.*

"Ah c'est vraiment gentille," the old Transylvanian vampire is smiling. More and more, she notices, people find it remarkably easy to say no to her. They say no without even saying it, the way they used to say yes. Only Jackie still says yes without saying it. She says it swearing and growling, like a man. If only there was still a man to swear and growl and give in. A man with money would be a lot more use to her than this clumsy, too-big woman who has left her son. She wouldn't even say why, but Ruth knew why. It was nothing she could say, either, but she sensed it. It was a failure on Jackie's part to accept men for the way they were, with all their limitations. To compromise, the way one did with men. To let them bluster, soothe and administer, and then to demand one's reward in kind. In shoes like soft, pleated suede shells. In holidays, and food from Selfridges's Food Halls. That was how it worked, with men. But Jackie refused the bargain. She wanted something from them they could never give. Well, she had a new one, now. Let her find out. As for Daniel, he had another woman, too. Ruth sighs. She cannot warm to the other woman, even though she has money. But she must organise herself. Where were her gloves, her glasses and her keys? She bumbles around the flat in a flurry of activity while Jackie scowls.

She's thinking of the last time she took Ruth to the cinema. They spent the entire time looking for her fur toque which they found when the lights came up at the end, under her seat. She had to grit her teeth to keep from smacking the old baby. There was the time she took her to the Mass of the Easter Vigil at the French church in Leicester Square. Jackie remembered the Easter Mass as stirring, pagan, a celebration of water and new fire. She felt in need of inspiration. Ruth is Jewish but she loves religion, period. She was delighted to come. Jackie felt positively sanctified. But then Ruth hissed in her ear the whole time, and she wanted to kill the old lady. Set her on fire with the Paschal candle, drown her in a well of cold new water. Time spent with Ruth was always a kind of total immersion in her element, her world. You went back in time. You lived in a novel by Colette. Jackie adores Colette, but her novels are hell to live in, especially when someone else is playing the Colette part. You get to be one of the minor parts, a grotesque.

"Remember, Ruth," she warns her sternly. "Afterwards, we are going to John Lewis's to get the Ecco shoes the doctor says you need."

"Oh, they are so ugly." Ruth can find nothing. She wants to cry. She can't remember eating today. Some bread maybe, with her coffee. It's so much trouble to cook, and the meals the home help makes will poison her if she eats them. Horrible English food her stomach can't digest. Her stomach digests French, Rumanian, Hungarian, German, Spanish, Italian, all the languages she speaks. Really, she should have been an interpreter. Only English, she cannot digest.

"There's the taxi. Let's get this show on the road," Jackie says impatiently. What has the old bat lost now? Why does she have to fumble and claw at things and make such a big production out of everything? It's exactly like getting a baby ready to go out. A nightmare. At least babies pretty much pass out once you hit the fresh air. This one goes on complaining.

"I am not ready," Ruth says in terror, her voice sharp with distress. "I have not my gloves, the keys - I cannot go out without them. If I bother the porter again, he will kill me."

Good job. Jackie hunts, finds. Minutes later, sweaty and thrumming with irritation, she more or less pushes Ruth out of the flat and watches her bolt the door's three locks with exasperated sympathy. Ruth is almost blind. Not quite. Tiny all her life, she's shrivelled to the size Jackie was, she gauges, at about age twelve. She battles with the keys and Jackie lets her, standing back and pretending a patience she not only doesn't feel but has never felt. The pretence is important. Ruth must be allowed to lock and unlock her own front door, however long it takes her. Otherwise she'll lose all pretence of independence. That pretence is even more important.

"Daniel goes mad when I do zat," Ruth says as she finishes. "He is so impatient."

Jackie opens the door for her and smiles crankily as she helps her inside. Ruth can slag her son off as much as she likes, it changes nothing. She knows all his fault, and he's the love of her life. But it's a small victory for her to compare well with her ex-husband in the matter of patience, when really neither of them has the smallest bit of it. They have many faults in common. Too many.

She is sinking about Daniel, Ruth surmises as the door slams and they sail off. The big black taxis are the best thing about London. *She misses him now, so stupid.* In her day it was the men who left, like her husband. The women missed them, like she does even now. That was normal. But for a woman to leave someone and then miss them, that was really stupid. These women with all their freedom, they were no more smart than she was. That cheers her up, and she starts looking forward to the shop and the shoes.

"John Lewis's," Jackie reminds her again. "We're not skipping it, Ruth. No arguments."

"You can wear flat shoes, you are tall," Ruth looks at her ex-daughter-in-law's feet. Sandals like Jesus wore are also not for women. But when one's feet are so big, what does it matter what one wears? *Elle est grande comme Gargantua,* she told her son when he brought her home. She was too big for him, it was true. Now Ruth tried to think who wrote *Gargantua,* but she cannot. It gets tangled up with Pascal and Candide and Pantagruel. She was educated at Grenoble like all wealthy young Rumanian ladies of her generation, and now she remembers nothing. She could ask Jacqueline, such a lovely name. Horrible, broken down to Jackie. But they are at Ferragamo. The doorman in his uniform helps her inside, giving her his arm so that her cane is unnecessary, a toy.

Like somesing for Marlene Dietrich or Maurice Chevalier, she says to him laughing, flirting a little. It feels so good to be touched by a man again. Like that, protectively. To be handed up the steps. Such a gentleman, the doorman. Perhaps if one had married a man in uniform? Not a doorman, of course, but an officer.

Ah, but now she is in the shop and she forgets this man, all men. The shoes are so beautiful, hand-stitched in softest leather. They all have heels, of course, at least the ones that interest her. Even the flats do not offend her, not here.

I feel like fucking Gulliver in here. Jackie moves around carefully, afraid of upsetting displays. There is not a single pair of shoes in the whole place that would fit her. *I'd have to wear them on my hands and walk upside down.* Ruth looks like she's seeing the Beatific Vision as she walks around smiling, touching the shoes. No one minds.

You're supposed to touch them. Everyone in here has clean hands. Her own hands feel sweaty. They might leave a stain on the soft leather or suede. Ruth has attracted a salesman, she's trying on shoes. Silly cow, she can't afford them. There isn't a pair of shoes in here for under a hundred pounds.

Ruth wills her daughter-in-law to let her be. Sometimes she leaves off the 'ex'. Everything is ex, at her age. Expatriate, she and Jackie are both that. Besides, you put an ex in front of something, what difference does it make? None. She tries on the soft beige heels, rising from her chair with the salesman's discreet help and parading slowly in front of the shining mirrors. She could almost dance in shoes like these. It's like being barefoot on warm sand. She still has the expensive dancing shoes from Budapest, from Bucharest, from Zurich and Geneva and Paris. How she danced. Dancing was more to her taste than sex. *If only you could get pregnant by dancing,* she said to her sister long ago. It seemed ingenious until Lisa reminded her about overpopulation. A special dance, she answered, not to be daunted. *A special dance they teach to people only when they marry.*

"They're lovely," Jackie is saying, standing next to her. "But dangerous for you, Ruth. Look at that heel."

She storms back to the striped silk seat of the white upholstered chair she'd like to lift up to her shoulder and carry away to her flat. *Dangerous.* What was dangerous was being wayward and wilful and leaving husbands before they could leave you. She tries on another pair, defiantly. *These shoes,* she holds one up and looks at it, *these shoes remind me I was young. They talk to me about going to the theatre and the ballet and to restaurants and laughing in the faces of young, handsome men.* She watches her own feet walk forward in the soft, shining shoes, but it is as if she's walking backwards into rooms lighted with chandeliers and candles. The Ferragamo mirrors have a lustre to them like candlelight, but sharper, like the prisms of the crystal chandeliers. All those things have gone out of her life. Big, shining cities, not grey and gloomy like this one. Theatres and dances and restaurants and magic light. She sits down, tired.

"Time to go, Ruth," Jackie says a little more sharply than she intends. This place sets her teeth on edge. It's the teeny tiny shoes and the teeny tiny women like Ruth, chic and continental and scary. She used to be petrified of Ruth. Daniel's mother was so utterly European, so elegant that when she went to Paris on the boat-train in the old days, her luggage was invariably searched by Customs when she came back. She looked like a mistress of someone important, or a spy.

"Time to go," Ruth agrees sadly. She puts on her own ancient, well-preserved Bali pumps. The salesman helps her with the tiny buckles, impeccably polite.

"Another time, madam," he says.

"I wish there would be another time," she says, and means it. The doorman helps her down the steps and doffs his top hat to her. She smiles with gracious exhaustion she knows from experience that no amount of rest will cure.

"I want to go to John Lewis's," she says to Jackie. "It's such a nice day, and an ordinary taxi is so expensive."

Jackie nods. *Oh let her walk,* she thinks wearily. It's like staving off an execution. Ruth scans the window of every single shoe shop between Bond Street and Oxford Street, and there are many. She pronounces judgement on every pair of heels. The flats are beneath her contempt. But none of the shoes, however they try, can hold a candle to Ferragamo. That's the phrase she keeps echoing in each chill, glassy entranceway she steps out of the sunlight to pace. *Nosing can hold a candle to the Ferragamos.*

The shoe department at John Lewis's is on the fifth floor. They take the elevator and Ruth sits in an infinitely less silken and elegant chair, as Jackie tells the woman what she doesn't want. When the Ecco shoes are lifted from the plain white box, she groans aloud, and the clerk and Jackie both laugh.

"Walk in them, Ruth," Jackie directs her. "See how comfortable they are."

The Ecco shoes are green. They say *old, sick, ugly* to her as she walks along. You do not walk the same way in flat shoes. That sense of elevation, that feminine poise, is gone. *I am no more a woman,* she thinks, looking down. Anyone could wear these shoes. A child, a man. Her heart cries out against such sexual anonymity. *My shoes are all I have left.* The men are gone. Now it is only the old but still fine shoes from Bali and Chanel and Ferragamo hanging papoose-fashion from her wardrobe door that echo her own female footsteps as she walks along in them. But she has fallen, twice.

She stomps up and down the shoe department of John Lewis's on ugly, functional green carpet that matches the ugly, functional green shoes. She cannot reconcile herself to this. She has lost most of her eyesight, most of her mobility, most of her friends and most of her hope. She cannot read any more, her son comes for lightning visits that last fifteen minutes if she's lucky, her beloved twins come less and less, Jonathan never, Joshua, who was so faithful, more, but still less than before. The last three or four times he visited they drank wine, which he likes, and she found herself begging him to help her kill herself. Daniel was bitterly angry with her, and Jackie said she must not do that again.

But she has gone on from all that, in her prolonged twilight. *Only this is too much.* Illness, stroke, blindness, loneliness that makes her heart howl like a dog, yes, disappointment with and for her own beloved son whose career has never quite reached the golden heights she craved for him. All that she can survive, but not this. She walks stiffly, angrily, while Jackie and the woman stand laughing at her. *Let them laugh. Their turn will come.*

"Shoes say everything about women," Jackie sighs philosophically to the clerk. She hates this. It's too painful, too guilt-forming, too sad. Ruth needs a miracle to save her from the Ecco shoes. "Young women wear those big lace-up boots now, with dresses and everything. I can't get my head round those."

The woman nods politely, but it's not really her head she can't get into a pair of huge, clunky Doc' Martens. It's her big American feet. Sandals make them even bigger, probably, but she's used to them. Ruth stomps back eventually and plops her small self as inelegantly as she can into the surly chair.

"Take zem off," she instructs the woman peremptorily. This one is not so nice, not like the men at Ferragamo. Besides, she hates being waited on by women.

"Ruth,' Jackie says under her breath. She hates it when Ruth gets on her high horse. She does it with nurses in hospitals, too. Never with doctors, of course.

"They fit all right, don't they," Jackie continues.

"Zey fit," Ruth says grimly. "Like the boots the Nazis wore."

"Ruth!" But she can't help laughing. The woman is laughing, too. They take the shoes over to pay for them and Ruth hands over forty pounds, with shaking hands.

"I have to pay to suffer," she says to no one in particular and then, to the woman behind the till, "If zey don't fit, I can return zem?"

"But they do fit," Jackie admonishes her. "They fit perfectly." She catches them a cab outside the store and they trawl home to a cup of tea and then her own negotiated parole. Actually, she decides after she's sprung, out on the pavement in the fading evening, Ruth makes it easier by making it so difficult. By the time you finish listening to her whine and wheedle and complain and bribe, you're ready to wallop her with a baseball bat and make a run for it.

Ruth puts the box of green shoes deep in her wardrobe. No papoose treatment for them. She forgets where they are, until Daniel demands to see them. Threatened with having to wear them and listen to them tell her, *Death is dark green and ugly but we are even uglier and we are you,* she walks all the way to John Lewis's with them, alone, and returns them. On her way home she loses the forty pounds and Daniel is so coldly furious with her he takes her back to buy another pair and makes her wear them out of the store. Once she begged to wear fragile, lovely dancing pumps home from the store and her mother laughed and agreed indulgently. It was an excuse to get a taxi, which they both enjoyed. She stuck out her feet in front of her and admired them, all the way home. She and Daniel do not enjoy the silent ride, and she tried not to look at her horrible feet. Mortified, she looks out the window at other people's shoes. Once home she takes them off and they have another row, but Daniel is too eager to get away to insist on anything but that she keep them this time, which she promises to do.

Mortified. She thinks the word, stomping out of her flat on the Ecco shoes. Her friend Jana who lives next door, the Hungarian whore, she will laugh when she sees them. Actually she is a retired madam, and very comfortably retired, too. They are friends now but often they have fallings out, and the last time Jana dined with her, she said that Ruth had poisoned her. They didn't speak for six months over that. But now they are on speaking terms, only luckily not today.

Mortified. She studied in Grenoble. She knows the root. The green shoes are killing her. She is like the wicked witch who danced to death in red shoes in the fairy tale, only that would be better. The shoes were hot, molten, and the death was quick. These are just ugly green shoes, like wearing mould on her feet. She will wear the mould and not the shoes. Thanks heaven Jews are buried without shoes, otherwise she might spend eternity in them. Jana will know. Old whores know everything about sex and death. She has told all her sex stories a million times. Let her tell some death ones.

She will invite her over for stuffed vine leaves. It takes three days to make them properly, but it will be worth it. She'll tell what no one else will, this woman of easy virtues. Jackie laughs when she hears Ruth call her that. *Let her laugh.* There were no more women of virtues, easy or not easy. Not herself, either. What she is doing is forbidden by God. But to have virtues one must have a little pleasure in life. One must have pleasures in food and drink, not too much. Even holy ones had that, even in a drop of water. One must have echo shoes from Ferragamo like white shells held to the ear. *One must have what one must have,* she says to all the men in her mind like judges. When one can have it no more, *c'est fini.* Or, as she tends to put it to herself, *I am finito.* She will take the taxi to Selfridges's and back again so she can shop without putting the horrors on her feet.

Then she will cook. She buries the Ecco shoes in her closet again. There is no one she hates enough to leave them to. Enemies dic, just like friends. Let them go to Oxfam, let them go to hell. She marches delicately towards the phone, black patent leather court shoes gleaming, to ring the knowledgeable old ex-madam and the taxi.

LIST OF CONTRIBUTORS

EDWARD BOYNE lives and works in Dublin. He has had poetry and several short stories published and broadcast. He is completing his first novel.

MICHAEL CARSON was born in Wallasey in 1946. He has written nine novels, including *Sucking Sherbet Lemons* and *Hubbies*, as well as a collection of short stories, *Serving Suggestions*. Based in a cottage in County Mayo, he has been lecturing in Imaginative Writing at Liverpool John Moores University for the last two years.

EDMUND CUSICK lectures in Imaginative Writing at Liverpool John Moores University. He co-edited and contributeds to *The Writer's Workbook* and has collaborated with Ann Gray to jointly publish a volume of poetry, *Gronw's Stone* (Headland Publications).

ROBERT DOYLE is 28 years old and lives in Ainsdale. He is an Ph. D student at Liverpool John Moores University and is writing a novel about perverts.

JAMES FRIEL lectures in Imaginative Writing at Liverpool John Moores University. He is the author of *Left of North*, *Taking the Veil* and *Careless Talk*. He has also adapted *Cousin Bette*, *Villette*, *As I Lay Dying* and *Saigon* for BBC Radio.

ROBERT GRAHAM teaches writing at Edge Hill, Ormskirk. He is the author, with Keith Baty, of *Elvis - The Novel*, (The Do-Not Press, 1997). *If You Have Five Seconds To Spare*, his play about fans of The Smiths, was produced by Contact Theatre, Manchester in 1989. His stories have appeared in various magazines and on BBC Radio 4. He is currently finishing a novel, *Holy Joe*.

PAULA GUEST was born in Liverpool in 1961 and now lives in Warrington. She is a prize-winning short story writer and her work has been broadcast on BBC Radio. *Parallel Worlds* was shortlisted in the 1999 South and Mid-Wales Writers' Association Mathew Pritchard Competition and her short play was a winner in the Everyman Theatre's New Voices Competition. Paula has recently completed an MA in Writing at Liverpool John Moores University and is currently working on her first novel.

PENNY KILEY is a former rock journalist now freelancing as a wordsmith of all trades (theatre criticism, copy editing, PR). She has been published in *Melody Maker*, *Smash Hits*, *Liverpool Daily Post & Echo*, *The Rough Guide to Rock* and *Mslexia*. She has just completed an MA in Writing at Liverpool John Moores University.

AILEEN LA TOURETTE has unleashed on the world *Nuns and Mothers* and *Cry Wolf* from Virago Press and *Weddings and Funerals*, short stories with Sara Maitland from Brilliance Books. Her short stories have been included in anthologies here and in the US, most recently in *The Mammoth Book of Lesbian Short Stories*, Canada and UK, 1998. Her most recent radio play was *My Darling My darling My Life and My Bride*, about the death of Edgar Allen Poe. She lectures in Imaginative Writing at Liverpool John Moores University and is currently working on a collection of poems entitled *Downward Mobility* and a trilogy of novels. She has two grown-up sons and lives on the Wirral Peninsula.

HEATHER LEACH now writes and teaches, but has also worked as a driver, clerk, youth and community worker and mother. She has had short stories published in a number of magazines and anthologies, including *Northern Stories*, *The Big Issue* and *The City Life Book of Manchester Short Stories*. She is currently working on her first novel.

OWEN LIDDINGTON was born in 1978 and brought up in North Wales. He is now studying Literature and Imaginative Writing at Liverpool John Moores University where he is completing a collection of short stories.

JANE MCNULTY was born in Cadishead, a former steel town to the west of Manchester, in 1955. She has won prizes for her short stories and poetry as well as the Liverpool John Moores University Lynda La Plante Award for a screenplay. A former biker, adventure playleader, bar-maid and community economic development worker, she now hopes to write for television. She is married with two children, and shares her home with various pets and her collection of Ray Lowry original artwork.

HELEN NEWALL'S earliest ambition was to be a writer. She's taken a round about route via fringe theatre and teaching in Africa and now writes plays for young people. She has an MA in Writing and is working on a PhD. She is currently Writer in Residence at the HTV-West Television Workshop in Bristol.

JENNY NEWMAN is the editor of *The Faber Book of Seductions* (1988) and co-editor of *Women Talk Sex: autobiographical writing about sex, sexuality and sexual identity* (Scarlet Press, 1992). She has also written two novels, *Going In* (Penguin, 1995) and *Life Class* (Chatto & Windus, 1999), and many articles on contemporary British writing. She is currently Head of Liverpool John Moores Centre for Writing.

NEIL O'DONNELL was born in Manchester in 1975. Having travelled and completed a Literature and Imaginative Writing degree at Liverpool John Moores University, he intends to continue avoiding responsibility. He is currently researching his first novel.

CAROL SMITH is a Scot living and working in Liverpool. She confesses to an intense childhood love affair with cinema travelogues. She has lived in Europe and the Far East. She has given up stuttering through Shakespeare.

JAKE WEBB was born in Harlow in 1977 and has since lived in Ahvaz, Bogota, Dallas and Liverpool. He now lives in Wiltshire. Other than writing, he likes listening to records, walking around, and taking note of extreme weather conditions.